CRUZ'S WATCH

BROTHERHOOD PROTECTORS WORLD

TEAM WATCHDOG
BOOK THREE

STACEY WILK

Twisted Page Press LLC

For Lynn
Thank you for the support and friendship.
Who knew a trip to the orthodontist could be so
fulfilling!

BROTHERHOOD PROTECTORS
ORIGINAL SERIES BY ELLE JAMES

Brotherhood Protectors Series

Fighting for Esme - Jen Talty
Fighting for Charli - Leanne Tyler
Fighting for Tessa - Stacey Wilk
Fighting for Kora - Deanna L. Rowley
Fighting for Fiona - Kris Norris

Athena Project
Beck's Six - Desiree Holt
Victoria's Six - Delilah Devlin
Cygny's Six - Reina Torres
Fay's Six - Jen Talty
Melody's Six - Regan Black

Team Trojan
Defending Sophie - Desiree Holt
Defending Evangeline - Delilah Devlin
Defending Casey - Reina Torres
Defending Sparrow - Jen Talty
Defending Avery - Regan Black

Brotherhood Protectors Yellowstone World
Team Wolf
Guarding Harper - Desiree Holt
Guarding Hannah - Delilah Devlin
Guarding Eris - Reina Torres
Guarding Payton - Jen Talty
Guarding Leah - Regan Black

Team Eagle

Booker's Mission - Kris Norris
Hunter's Mission - Kendall Talbot
Gunn's Mission - Delilah Devlin
Xavier's Mission - Lori Matthews
Wyatt's Mission - Jen Talty

CHAPTER 1

CRUZ LACERDA TOOK CALCULATED RISKS. Calculated risks minimized disaster and death. Risks taken on a whim caused destruction, oftentimes the kind that couldn't be returned from. Blame it on the education. Blame it on the former day job. But he needed to have as much information as possible before he could make a solid decision—about pretty much anything.

Which was why he had researched the Vortex Backpacker and their adventure hiking tours before booking a trip for him and his two longtime friends.

"I can't believe you talked us into this." Mason finished his coffee and motioned for the waitress to bring more. "How many more hikes are you going to go on?"

"As many as it takes." To get over his soon-to-be ex-wife. He just wasn't going to say that part.

He, Mason, and Ryder sat in the local eatery which shared the parking lot with the motor lodge that the three friends had stayed in last night. When he shifted in his seat, the vinyl booth held together with duct tape squeaked beneath him. His fingers stuck to the laminate tabletop, but the coffee was good.

Before the sun hung full in the sky they would climb onto the school bus—no longer yellow but sporting a faded and pocked forest green—that would take them to the start of the four-day extreme hike.

"I think I want to beat you for this. It's too early to be up." Ryder wiped a hand over his face and shook his head as if he could force the sleep from his brain. "Aren't you tired of early morning hikes? Didn't you get enough of that in the Air Force?"

"Come on, guys. Hiking keeps you young." He had asked them six months ago to accompany him on this adventure hike. He needed something to look forward to and something that would challenge him.

For the past sixteen months, he had tried to shut out his problems, but nothing took, not work, not his new job with the Brotherhood Protectors, not vacations, not women. Hiking was the only thing that gave him any reprieve. He craved more hikes and ones that pushed him so hard he wanted to crumble.

"Sleep keeps you young too, and the experts recommend you do it while it's still dark out." Ryder looked into his coffee cup and sighed. "It's empty." He motioned for the waitress to pour him more too.

"Here's the check, boys. Sadie will take it at the counter." The waitress, whose name tag read Angelica, plopped down the handwritten order complete with her number and a little heart, floating off the last digit. She glided away with a subtle glance over her shoulder.

"Who is the number for?" Ryder flipped the paper over as if it held the answer.

"She likes your sorry ass." Mason grabbed the receipt, slid out of the booth, and wandered over to the cashier.

"Not me. It's you, Lacerda. It's that dark skin. Very sexy." Ryder wiggled his fingers in Cruz's face.

"Knock it off." He pushed Ryder's hands away. Ryder burst out laughing.

"I'm not interested. You call her." Of course, he wasn't interested. His divorce wasn't final, and relationships weren't his thing at the moment.

He pushed out of the booth too, ready to get this adventure started. Four days in the wilderness, no cell phones, no distractions from the outside world. No phone calls or text messages from his soon-to-be ex-wife.

"Maybe I will give her a call." Ryder hustled over to Mason and took the paper back.

Cruz grabbed his backpack and pushed out into the early morning air. The sun would be up soon, bringing with it rising temperatures. The mountain elevation would keep them cool since it was July. Hiking in oppressive heat and humidity wasn't good for anyone.

The bus idled in the lot, coughing its exhaust everywhere. Other hikers boarded. Some sipped what was most likely high-octane coffee. Others chatted with friends in an excited, chipmunk-like manner. These four days would clear his head. He didn't have to think about anything other than the wilderness around them. He would analyze the weather—a hazard of his job as a meteorologist and former combat weatherman—but without cell service, he couldn't check any radar monitors.

"You ready?" Mason patted him on the shoulder.

He could barely remember a time that Mason and Ryder weren't by his side. He had met them in a pickup hockey game when they were kids back in Buffalo. Mason and Ryder were already friends back then, but they had added Cruz into their fold without hesitation, and they had stayed friends ever since. They remained friends when he had gone to college in Colorado. They were in the Air Force together. Mason and Ryder had been groomsmen at his wedding.

He silently groaned. He needed to stop thinking about being married to Ayla.

"Yeah, I'm ready. More ready than I realized."

"Is there any chance we can talk you out of this?" Ryder hoisted his pack onto his back.

"You know you're going to love it, Callahan. Any excuse for you to help a lady in distress. And by the looks of those two, you'll get a chance." He pointed to two women waiting near the bus with their heads huddled together over a phone. One wore pink sweatpants with a matching cropped sweatshirt. The hood was outlined in fake pink fur. The other looked as if she was ready for a yoga class and not a hike. Both wore the wrong kind of shoes.

"Not my type." Ryder looked back at the pair.

"Mine either," Mason said.

"Seriously? Isabella?" He gave Mason a shove.

"Yeah, yeah. I know. Never say never." Mason shoved him back.

"What's the weather forecast for this trip?" Ryder secured his pack in place with the waist belt.

"I didn't look." He hadn't. It was a first for him. He was trying to be more relaxed.

"Yeah, right. This is you, Lacerda. You check the weather before you take a leak. How many times have you told us not to fly because the weather was bad? Or not to ski?" Mason said.

"I'm saving your life, dumbass." His phone rang and startled him. "Forgot to turn it off." He dug the phone out of his pants pocket and groaned out loud this time. "It's Ayla."

"Answer it," Ryder said.

"I can't."

"You need to talk to her." Mason grabbed his phone and tapped the screen.

He lunged to get it back before Mason could say anything, but he jumped out of Cruz's reach. Ryder slapped his leg and laughed. Cruz shot him a glare, but it did nothing to shut up Ryder.

"Hey, Ayla. It's Mason."

"I'm going to kill you." This trip was supposed to be about getting Ayla off his mind and Mason knew that. Answering that call would stir up trouble. He should walk away, get on the bus, and let Mason deal with Ayla and her latest issue. Though his curiosity was piqued. Why was she calling so early?

"Yeah, he's here. I saw it was you calling and wanted to say hello." Mason paused. Ayla must have started talking.

"Sure. Sure. I'll put him on." Mason handed him the phone. "She sounds upset."

She probably was. Ayla was often upset with him. "Thanks." He took the phone and stepped away to the opposite side of the parking lot and out of earshot.

"Hey, Ayla." He took a slow breath to brace himself for what was about to pummel him like a Category 5 hurricane.

"Cruz, the basement flooded. I don't know what to do." Her frantic voice crossed the line and seared his heart.

How many times had he come to her rescue, this woman who leaped before she thought about how far she would fall. Who, he was almost certain, married him as if he were a dare more than the fact she may have loved him. Ayla always ended up tangled in a dramatic mess she didn't know how she found herself in, as if she stumbled and fell without her consent.

"Do you know where the water is coming from?" He should tell her to call someone else, that he was no longer responsible for cleaning up her fallout.

The tour guide, Dexter, waved from the door of the bus to the hikers still milling around. Most looked in Dexter's direction, except for the two women still staring at that phone, and shuffled their feet to climb aboard. Mason and Ryder gawked at him. Mason held his hands up as if to say *what gives?* He flashed them a one-minute signal.

"The ground. It seeped right in and ruined my photos and a whole bunch of other stuff," Ayla said, dragging his attention away from his friends and the people on the bus.

"What did you say?" He turned away from the bus again to focus on this conversation and end it as soon as possible.

"It's been raining for days. The basement flooded. What do I do?" Mingled with the rise of her voice was a crinkling sound as if she opened a plastic bag. He didn't ask what she was doing. It could be anything from making toast to throwing out old dry-cleaning bags.

"You'll have to bail it out. When the ground dries and the rain stops, the water will go away. Then call the landscaper like I told you to and have them come regrade the landscaping around the house." They had been over this a dozen times in the past year. He had suggested they sell the house, but Ayla wanted to stay there. He didn't argue. He wanted the divorce to be as amicable as possible and for her to be comfortable.

"But everything is ruined."

"I can't help you with that. I have to run. I'm sorry." He glanced back at the bus. Dexter tapped his wrist as if to say Cruz was wasting time. Mason and Ryder waited outside the bus for him.

"Wait. Don't go yet. I need your help."

"I have an appointment."

"Cruz, please. Our wedding photos are destroyed."

"They're just photos. You weren't planning on keeping them, were you?" He didn't understand what she was so upset about. They were married twelve years ago, almost thirteen now. Neither one of them had looked at those photos in a long time. Maybe that should have been a sign.

"Lacerda, we've got to go." Ryder jogged over. "That Dexter kid is getting pissed. You're holding up the bus."

"Was that Ryder? Where are you three going?"

"Ayla, I don't have time for this. I have to go."

"Please. I wouldn't ask you if it wasn't important. You're the only one who knows how to fix things like this. When I saw our photos warped and swelling, the only thing I have left from our time together, I knew I needed to see you one more time."

"What do you mean one more time?" He tried to discern what hidden message was behind her statement, but with Ayla it could be anything.

"Before the divorce is final."

Okay, not what he assumed she was getting at and relieved that she wasn't. Ryder tugged on his arm, but all he could do was shake his head. He needed another minute or two to get his head around this call. She needed to see him. There could be a million reasons why, and he didn't have the time to sift through them.

"They're just photos. I'll call you when I get

9

back." He should not promise such a thing. He needed her to take care of the house problems without him now.

"Not to me they aren't. I promise to take care of the landscaping. Please can you help me? I don't have anyone else."

She knew what buttons to push on him and often did. Ayla didn't have a close family like his and her job kept her on the road a lot, making close friends a hard thing to maintain. Her impulsiveness often broke apart her work teams, leaving her stranded—sometimes literally.

He hated that she was alone, and she used his caring to her advantage. Separating from her had meant she might struggle without close ties. He didn't want that for her, but she had done the one thing he had asked her not to—the one thing—and left him little choice. She changed their lives forever. He couldn't come back from that, even though he had tried a million different ways.

"Let's go." Mason stood on the bus's bottom step now and waved him and Ryder over. Ryder arched a brow and jogged back to the bus.

"They're waiting for me, Ayla." The words hurt to say because a piece of him wanted to rescue her. He had liked being needed for a very long time, but when he needed someone to save him, she wasn't there. She had wanted to be and tried, but in the end, she let him down.

He would never get over her entirely. At least not in the near future. Every date he'd been on since their split had made that as clear as a summer sky.

"I understand. I do. I shouldn't have called. Old habits. You should go be with your friends. Take care." She put on her brave voice. He recognized the steeliness she used to prove she was fine on her own.

"Thanks. I'll check in with you when I get back in a few days. I'll help you dry out the basement. You take care too." He hesitated to end their conversation in case she had anything else to say, but only silence came back to him. "Ayla?" He checked the screen. The call had ended and he wondered if she hung up before he had finished.

He shoved his phone in his pocket and hurried to the bus. Dexter stood by the driver and glared at him. "I keep a tight schedule, Mr. Lacerda. If it wasn't for your two menacing friends, this bus would've left without you."

"I'm sorry. It's not my habit to be late. I had a family issue." He stumbled against the word family. Ayla had been part of his family since they were in college and now she was alone, standing in a foot of water—or worse, he had forgotten to check—and asking for his help.

He stepped onto the bus and stared down the aisle at the annoyed hikers more than ready to get their adventure started. They would all dislike him for this, and it would take most of the trip to win their trust. He would feel the same way if someone else had held him up. He had been ready to leave hours ago.

"Mason, Ryder, can you come here a minute?" He stepped off the bus and waited by the door.

"You have got to be kidding me right now." Dexter threw his skinny arms into the air and blew out a gust of wind from those thin lips of his. Dexter couldn't be more than twenty-five or had aged better than anyone Cruz had ever seen. Dexter wasn't old enough to know the complicated knot marriage could become and the constant struggle to wonder if he was doing the right thing by going or staying.

"What's up?" Mason trotted down the steps and stood beside him. Ryder joined them a second later.

"It's Ayla. She's in trouble and wants me to come help her."

"So go," Ryder said.

"But this trip is about to start and it's not major trouble like a health condition or her roof blew off. It's Ayla trouble." Which was code for if she ever planned more than ten minutes out, she wouldn't find herself ankle deep in water. He used to love that about her once, when they were kids in college. She would close her books while they were supposed to be studying and decide on a new adventure in that minute. Like the crazed, lovesick fool he was, he'd follow her. But after years of chasing Ayla like she was some tornado to be documented, but never tamed, the quest wore him out.

"Forget the trip, man. She's your wife, and she needs you. You'd come if it were one of us." Ryder gripped his shoulder and gave a shake. A solemn look passed over his face.

Ryder had been shocked when Cruz announced he left Ayla. He tried to convince him to stay, because he cared for Ayla almost as much as Cruz did, always telling him that he needed Ayla's spirit to balance him out. But he had been determined to get space from all the pain. At the time, it seemed to be the right idea.

"Soon-to-be ex-wife." The divorce train was in full force, like a winter storm already dumping inches of snow. Once it started, there was no going back, only forward.

"Never mind that. Go to her," Ryder said.

"I hate to agree with Callahan over here, because you know he's usually talking out of his ass, but he has a point." Mason shoved his hands in his pockets.

He looked between Mason and Ryder. He had trusted his life to these men in more combats than he cared to think about. Before their time in the service, these two had been by his side like brothers. Mason and Ryder agreed without hesitation to join the Brotherhood with him where he would act as their weather specialist for high-end clients who needed protection while flying or traveling long distances. They always talked straight with him, never blowing smoke up his ass and always calling him on his bullshit.

"I'm sorry about the trip." He unhooked his pack.

"You will owe us, sending us on this dumbass adventure without you, but go to her," Mason said.

"Thanks. Can you explain it to Dexter?"

"Yeah, we'll take care of Poindexter." Ryder choked out a laugh.

"Don't torture him too much." He shook hands with his friends and hurried to his truck. "The beers will be on me when you get back," he called after his friends.

"Damn straight," Ryder said.

"Never doubted that. Say hi to Ayla," Mason said, heading toward the bus.

"Will do."

He would go to Ayla's, get the water situation under control, and then leave. He wouldn't get caught up in anything else. His weekend getaway was ruined, and he would have to find some other way to work out the crap in his head.

Cruz slid into his truck and kicked over the engine. He pulled out of the lot before the bus. A quick glance in the rearview mirror showed Dexter throwing his hands in the air while Ryder and Mason stood beside him, both with grins on their faces, shaking their heads.

"Sorry, old boy. If you're ever in love, you'll understand."

His words stopped his breath. He was not still in love with his wife. But he would let her know he had rethought his decision about coming and tapped her name on his recent calls screen.

She picked up on the third ring. "Cruz?"

"I've changed my plans. I'm coming to help out, but this is the last time." He meant it. He had to start living his life without her. She could not keep calling him to save her, or he would never get over her.

"Definitely. Yes. I promise. And… thank you."

"Thank me later. I'll see you in a couple of hours." He tried not to picture the small smile that would tug on her lips when she got her way, especially from him.

"See you." She ended the call.

Still loving that woman he was about to divorce would be as crazy as chasing tornados.

"So why are you going?" he said to himself.

For the rest of the ride, that was a question he would not answer.

CHAPTER 2

AYLA LAID OUT the sopping wedding photos across the kitchen table and all the available counter space in the small house in Aurora that she and Cruz bought several years ago.

She had fallen in love with the open floor plan and original hardwood floors, but it was the wraparound porch that had stolen her heart.

The house faced east. She could sit on the porch with a giant cup of coffee and watch the sun rise with its long rays that shook the day awake, or the pregnant clouds that glided out to the plains, desperately wanting to rid the heavy weight they carried. Then at night, she could sit on the back deck that Cruz had built for her and watch the setting sun wrap the sky in shades of pinks and reds like a present just for her. But she would watch any weather—all weather.

The pictures were ruined, and she couldn't find the hard drive to have them replaced because she had boxed it up when she and Cruz had moved to this house. They had been married long enough that her wedding photos weren't on her current phone. They weren't even stored on a cloud. She had always meant to get around to uploading them, but never did. Now, she had nothing left of them except for the one photo they had framed and kept on the bedside table.

The photographs had been her domain. Cruz had wanted several photos printed and hung around the house, but she wouldn't let him take the photos anywhere to have it done. She had insisted she do it because she was the professional, and she would do a better job than anyone else. He hadn't argued that point, but he had implied she was busy and wouldn't have the time to get to it.

Like usual, Cruz had been right. She hated that about him. He was always right, and he tried like hell not to hang it over her head for most of their marriage. He had been right about her not chasing tornados too.

She hurried from the kitchen, needing space from the reminders of a happier life. She couldn't think about the day they married or the awful day when everything changed. Not now. Not when Cruz would be here any minute. She needed to ask him a favor which required her to be focused because he was more than likely going to say no, and she was out of options.

She jumped in the shower so she wouldn't smell like yesterday. He didn't need to see her with her bedhead and wearing one of his old t-shirts as a nightgown. She needed to look amazing so he could miss her, even if it was only for a minute.

The laundry basket was filled with clean clothes. None were folded so every article looked like an accordion, but she didn't have time to iron. She didn't even own an iron. Ironing was Cruz's domain. The retired lieutenant colonel wanted everything starched and pressed—like her father.

She opted for her green wide-leg linen pants that had black wispy flowers all over it and a white cropped tank top. She let her wild, kinky hair flow around her face. He liked it best that way. She slid on her beaded bracelets and slid off her wedding ring.

Of course, dressed in her good pants meant she couldn't wade in the basement water. The water wasn't as high as she had led Cruz to believe, but it was high enough to be a problem and she was desperate. He was the only person who could help her. She could have called a plumber maybe or the landscaper like Cruz had suggested, but she wanted to see him. It had been almost a year since they had been in the same place. They had communicated via texts mostly, which had been fine until she realized she missed him. Dumb, because he didn't miss her.

Her phone rang with the *Respect the Wind* ringtone. Someone was texting her. She hesitated to look. At the moment, there were not too many people she wanted to hear from. She approached the phone, buried under some of the photos as if it were a serpent about to strike. And it would if it was the director of the documentary awaiting her photos and videos because she was behind schedule and hadn't produced anything worthwhile. It could be her mother. She didn't have time to read that her mother wanted her to call more. Or one of her brothers, asking her when she was going to get a real job. Also like her father had.

The ringtone persisted, forcing her to grab the phone and face her fears. She wished facing all her fears were that easy. Her heart sank at the sight of the message.

You have one week to give me the footage you promised or we want our advance returned. Even without the benefit of his voice on the other line, she could imagine Foster Gillespie's high-pitched nasal tone filled with frustration and impatience toward her.

He could threaten all he wanted. She already spent the advance to pay her bills.

Foster had approached her before last year's tornado season to take photos and video of the supercells for his documentary series on extreme storms. She held up the project because she had been the one photographer who hadn't delivered. Now, this year's season was over. Tornados could happen any time of the year, but if she had wanted to document the most spectacular storms, her chances were better from April till June.

A series of storms are expected this week. You'll have what you need. She said a silent prayer before hitting send.

She hoped he would have what he wanted. Her luck had run out. Every storm behaved as if it knew she was after it and found ways to evade her. At least that's what she kept telling Foster. Instead of running toward the storms, she froze too far away to get anything worth sending to him. Every pep talk failed. Every threat failed. She could not get close enough to a tornado—maybe ever again.

If she didn't produce something of value right now, she might never get another chance. No one would hire her if Foster fired her. She had turned down so many opportunities to document severe weather, her reputation and business circled the drain—much like her marriage. She needed this win to come back, or she would have to return to taking school photos like she did when she was in college.

I had better. Keep me posted. Foster's text said much more than those few words. He could have added *or else* because that was what he would want to say to her.

Don't worry. I've got something lined up. She tossed the phone on the counter. What she had lined up was about to ring her doorbell. She only hoped he would agree.

~

Cruz PULLED into the driveway of the house he used to live in and technically still owned. The siding needed a good power wash. Some of the shutters pulled away from the house and would soon get caught by a strong wind and fall to the ground. Jagged weeds popped through the cracks in the cement and around the shrubbery under the front windows. He stifled a sigh and pushed out of the truck. His house needed some care.

He stretched out the kinks in his back and neck from the long drive over and wondered how Ryder and Mason made out on the bus ride to the start of the hiking spot. They should be there by now. He wished he was too.

The day heated up as the sun climbed into the sky—just like he predicted. This was the first day in several that the sun had been out. The inches of rain had hit high levels and that was why the basement flooded. It always did when that happened. Something he had meant to take care of before he moved out, but never got around to it.

The temps would be in the normal range for Aurora today. Nothing spectacular was expected like a high wind thunderstorm. After all the rain this area had the past two weeks, they deserved a little sunshine. As did the ground around his house —Ayla's house.

Once she secured the loan to buy him out, he would sign his half over to her. Until then, they owned the house together. He didn't care how long it would take for her to gather the money. He was in no rush. She made the mortgage payments. Good thing, or he wouldn't be able to afford his new cabin closer to Fool's Gold and his new job with the Brotherhood Protectors.

He rang the bell instead of walking inside. He had handed back his keys close to a year ago. Ayla had asked him to because he used to come inside as if he still lived there, and she had explained in no uncertain terms he was no longer allowed to do that. His name was on the deed. He should be able to enter his own home, but if he really thought about it, this was not his house. A financial responsibility to the mortgage company did not a home make.

The door flew open. He sucked in a breath. Ayla was the most beautiful woman he had ever seen. From the moment he met her on the college quad in her ripped jeans and graphic t-shirt that revealed a belly button piercing, every other woman had paled in comparison to her.

Her curly hair went on for miles. One errant curl fell over her nose and onto her lip. She blew it out of her way with a huff. Her tank top showed off the tattoo of butterflies and lilies over her shoulder. She had another tattoo on her side of a storm cloud, but it was too high up to see unless she had no shirt on to cover it. He shoved that thought away as quickly as it appeared. Thoughts like that had no business taunting him.

"Hey," he said for lack of something better.

"Thanks for coming." She stepped to the side and waved her arm to welcome him in. Her bracelets sang a soft tune as they moved with her.

He passed her, leaving enough space that they would not touch, but he caught a whiff of her earthy, after a good rain, scent. He always wanted to make love to her in the mud when he smelled her after a shower. The instinct rose now, but he had to squash it before he did something they would regret. She still had all her power over him, and he needed to get that under control.

"Let's see the basement."

"Do you want a coffee or something?" She closed the door, sealing him in and for a moment he pictured a black widow spider. Was she up to something? Ayla might be scattered at times, but she was brilliant and creative and knew what she wanted. Her drive made her good at taking photos and videos of moving weather, but it also drove her headfirst into trouble.

"No, thanks. I'll just help you clear out anything that needs to be removed. We can bail out the water with some buckets. Um… it's not really my business, but aren't you dressed kind of nice for hauling water?"

"Oh, this? I just threw it on. It will be fine." She went into the kitchen and he followed.

Their wedding photos were scattered around the table and the counters. She had hung some from a string in front of the window that looked out onto the backyard. The shots of them standing on the volcano and smiling at the camera stopped him in his tracks. That young couple standing with their heads together, smiling for the camera, had been happy once.

"Why are you keeping these?" His fingers grazed the corner of the photo of them walking toward their guests. They had one hand in the air as if in victory while their other hands were clasped together. Ayla's smile rivaled the brilliance of a lightning storm.

"I can't throw them out. Those are memories."

"Memories you would rather forget." The statement was out before he could stop it.

"You can't resist an opportunity to throw my

words in my face, can you?" She crossed her arms over her chest.

"I didn't come here to fight with you. I'm sorry I said anything. I'll go down into the basement and take care of the water. You can stay up here. When I'm done, I'll let you get back to whatever your weekend plans were."

He shrugged out of his denim shirt and tossed it over the chair. Ayla's gaze bored into him.

"I can help you."

"I don't need the help, but thank you." Having her too close to him would be a distraction. He would continue to inhale her scent and struggle to keep his hands to himself. She didn't want him that way anymore. Even if he took a crazy risk and told her that what he really wanted was to tear up the divorce papers and try again because he had been a fool to let her go, she would still turn him away. Ayla had made up her mind. He had helped.

"You don't think I can help you. You think I'll mess up your plan to clean the basement—which I am certain that you were orchestrating all the way over here. You have it figured out to the minute and the ounce of water you'll be carrying. If I get involved, you won't be able to control me."

"Ayla, please. I don't want to fight with you." She had him figured out. She always had. He couldn't hide from her. He had thought about the best way to get the water out of the basement and how quickly he could do it so he could get back on the road.

But he did not ever want to control her. Holding too tightly to Ayla was the equivalent of trying to wrap his hands around a southern wind. Only a fool would try that.

"I'm not fighting. I'm discussing." She blew that piece of hair away from her face again.

"By accusing me of controlling you?"

She stepped closer and grabbed a photo off the counter. "Do you remember this one?" she said, ignoring his last question.

He took the photo, and it stuck to his fingers. He remembered the moment well. Their wedding had been in Maui so his beautiful bride could have photos on an active volcano. What he wouldn't do for her back then. They had climbed down near the shore for this picture. The material on her head-piece had been long, so long that Ryder had stepped on it and almost tore it out of her head at one point during the day.

Cruz thought the piece was called the train, but he had never paid attention to those details. He had watched that volcano to make sure it didn't spew on them. But Ayla's train had slipped into the water, and she tried to pull it out and slipped.

He had grabbed her around her waist and tossed her over his shoulder in a fireman's carry. The motion had been instinctual more than anything because he hadn't wanted her to fall in and the photographer had snapped the shot at the exact right moment. They looked playful, but he had been scared. If she had fallen and hit her head... But she hadn't. He had tried to give up protecting her too, also a fool's journey, but that instinct remained in place.

"It was a good day." He handed the photo back.

"Do you ever think about it?" She took another step toward him, closing the space and confusing him with her nearness. Ever since he had walked out, the few times he was in her company—maybe once or twice—she had made it a point to keep a few feet between them whenever possible. Or maybe that had been him.

"Our wedding day? Why do you ask?"

She slid a hand onto his arm. Her cool touch against his heated skin sent a shock over him.

"I think about it." Her voice dipped an octave. "You made that whole day happen for me. You used to make all kinds of things happen for me."

"What's going on here?" He stepped away, and her hand fell to her side.

"Nothing. Unless you want it to." She looked up at him through her lashes.

He studied the scene. She was nicely dressed with a touch of gloss on her full lips. Their photos decorated the whole room as if they were an exhibit. She approached him with heat in her eyes.

"Are you coming on to me?"

She stepped back to her corner, the heat gone and replaced with a cool stare. "What if I was? Would that be so bad? We used to be good in bed."

"We were great in bed. Sex was never our problem. But we're not together anymore. Or did you forget?" He wanted to sleep with her because she was still the woman he thought about at night when he was alone. He wanted to take her to bed because his head was full of old memories that shouldn't be any good anymore, but were strong enough to taste.

"You wouldn't let me forget." She heaved a big sigh. "Look, the basement isn't that bad. There's water along that back wall like usual, but that vacuum thing that you left in the garage could probably suck it up."

Now he was very confused. "Are you saying you didn't need my help?"

"I do. But not with that."

The room tilted. He grabbed the counter to keep from falling on his ass. She had set him up for something, and he had fallen for her ruse. "I need to see the basement."

The door to the basement was in the mudroom off the kitchen. He would have to brush past her to get to it, but at this moment he didn't care about being too close to her. He needed to see for himself.

"Cruz, wait." She reached for him, but he dodged her.

They had finished the basement right after they had moved in by adding a beige Berber carpet, drywall with some insulation, a drop ceiling, and a pool table. The old sofa came later along with a flat-screen TV to watch sports. Ayla had confiscated a corner for all her photography equipment and computer.

He waited for the rancid smell of a wet basement and sopping carpet to assault him, but the air was clear. The carpet didn't squish under his feet until he got to the corner where several photo albums had been discarded on the floor as if the viewer had been taken away unexpectedly, leaving the albums behind for only a minute.

"Ayla," he said up the steps.

She stood in the doorway. The sun behind her painted her in a silhouette at the top of the steps. "Yes?"

"Were you looking at the photo albums and left them out? Is that why the wedding album was soaked?" Because there wasn't all that much water down here. It wasn't high enough to get onto the bookcase. Nothing else seemed to be wet either.

"Yes, Cruz. Would you like to give me the demerits now?" She huffed and walked away. The sun streamed down the steps and blinded him.

He took the steps two at a time. She stood on

the other side of the kitchen with her back to him. "Hey, hang on a second. Stop making me out to be the bad guy. You asked me to come out here because you needed my help. I left my hike to save you, and it appears there wasn't anything you needed to be saved from."

She spun on her heel. Her cheeks and neck bloomed red. "I exaggerated. I need you to help me with something else, and I knew you wouldn't come for that."

He did not want to think about what her real motive was. It didn't matter anyway. He would not get involved. She wasn't his concern any longer. Someone needed to let his heart in on the secret, that was all.

If he thought a simple conversation where he said he still loved her would fix this problem, he would have it with her. In fact, he had tried, but she had told him to go—in no uncertain terms. She did not want him any longer because he had left her. In reality, she had left him for the damn storm fronts.

He hadn't needed to be told twice and walked away for good. If he were being honest, for the longest time, when he thought about her, he saw hurt and loss. He had figured she was right about the end of them. A few weeks after that last talk, he had received the divorce papers and hired an attorney.

"I've got to go." If he hurried, maybe he could meet the guys somewhere along the way.

"Will you let me explain?"

"What's to explain? If you knew I didn't want to hear it before, what makes you think I'll listen now?" He grabbed his shirt off the chair.

"You're here."

"Was that why you tried to come on to me? Did you think if you got me in bed and waited until I was about to come to ask me for another crazy request that I'd be too high on you to say no?"

"No." She threw her hands in the air. "Well, maybe. But I hadn't thought about that until you were here. I swear. When you took off that shirt, and I saw your pecs under the t-shirt, I wanted to undress you completely and you know… jump you." Her lip twitched in a coy smile.

That woman craved sex more than a teenage boy. In the early years, he could not quench her thirst. As time went on and the decades passed, she slowed down and craved him less. Though he could come home from work and find her naked in the hallway or naked cooking dinner. If she wanted it in the middle of the night, she had woken him more than once.

"I don't even know what to say. I have to go."

He headed for the door.

"Please don't go." She hurried after him. "I need your help with work. If I don't get some decent footage, I'm going to lose my job. I can't lose my job. I won't get any others, and I need the money." She dropped her gaze to her bare feet.

He stopped with his hand on the knob. "You don't need me for that. You take good pictures and video. I would just get in your way. Plus, you have Austin to go with you."

"I don't have a partner anymore."

He almost asked why, but he didn't want to know. She would have a long story that would end with some version of *I couldn't help it*. "Why me?"

"Because you're the best at what you do."

"Are you saying what I think you're saying?" He was a retired combat weatherman. He had climbed the ranks inside the Air Force because he loved the weather and studying its patterns. He had saved lives because he could redirect a flight around a storm, amongst many other ways he had kept his teams alive. If Ayla wanted him to help her, it meant one thing.

"I need to chase a tornado."

"Hell no."

CHAPTER 3

AYLA STARED AT CRUZ, standing in the foyer with a death glare in his dark eyes. Even angry, he was incredibly handsome. He had grown in his hair some after he retired. The shaggy locks on the top of his head looked as if he had run his fingers through it, making her want to do the same.

But it was those dark, close-set, piercing eyes. His thick eyebrows gave him a constant quizzical look. Sometimes she wasn't sure if he was scrutinizing her or not. She should know this by now, but Cruz could be a mystery. His military training taught him to keep his emotions close. Nothing she had done had changed that about him. Her mother had told her trying to change Cruz was impossible. Ayla needed to love him as he was. And she had—until he left her. Problem was, she had left him first.

"We don't have to get too close to the storm. Just close enough so I can take video worth sending to my producer." She would promise him anything at this point.

She couldn't go out and chase alone. It wasn't smart. Better to have someone in the driver's seat so she could jump back in after the photos and videos were taken, and they would have a chance to get out of there before it was too late. Seconds counted in her line of work. No one knew that better than she did. Except maybe Cruz.

"Famous last words. I wasn't going to ask, but what happened to Austin?"

At least Cruz hadn't run for his truck, a good sign. She might have a chance to convince him. Asking him to come with her was a lot to expect from the man. Her career had stolen too much from him. She had lost plenty too, but she hadn't meant to bring him the kind of hurt she had.

"He got a better opportunity. He was worried about our track record and wanted out before the network fired us."

"That's it?"

"That's it." That wasn't all of it. Austin had left because she couldn't do the work. Every chase had her shaking and sweating. She had made him pull over once so she could hop out and have herself a good cry in the field. When Austin had found her there, sniffling and slobbering, he said she should find another line of work. He had asked to be reassigned the next day.

"Why a tornado?"

"I need the money."

"Where is all your money? I send you money every month from my paycheck and half my pension."

"I haven't been working. The network was worried about me."

"I don't understand. Did they have a reason to be?" He leaned against the wall and crossed his ankles.

No one wanted to work with the woman who had been in an accident. "First of all, I'm a woman in a man's field. Most of the guys don't want to work with me to begin with."

"I don't care about that part at the moment. I need to know if there were any other near misses? Did you go headfirst into trouble again?"

"I didn't go headfirst into trouble the last time. The tornado snuck up on me. My equipment wasn't giving me real-time information. No one had seen a tornado like that one." She tried to control the pitch of her voice. Even now, the memory was as real as it had been that day. She hadn't meant to get that close. The storm wasn't there and then it was. Her body still shook every time she remembered looking up and seeing the dark funnel as it tore up the ground right before her. She hadn't time to change directions. The draft caught her.

"I'm not blaming you. I never did."

"Yes, you did. You blamed me for everything. That was why you left."

"I left because I couldn't have a front row seat to the possibility of losing you anymore." He pushed off the wall. "Look, I'd better go. I don't think this will work out. You'll have to call someone else."

She reached for him but backed up as quickly. He couldn't be pressured. He would have to come to this idea on his own. "I don't have anyone else to call. I don't trust anyone else."

He stared off at the ceiling and wiped a hand over his face. The seconds ticked by as she waited for him to speak. She had spoken the truth about not trusting anyone else. Cruz was cautious and calculated his possibilities. He was probably doing that very thing while he stood in the foyer.

"What's the specific assignment?"

She tried to control the excitement taking flight in her belly and pressed her lips together to keep the smile from escaping. If Cruz asked questions, he was considering it. He was halfway to where she needed him.

"I have to produce footage for a documentary on extreme storms. I was offered the tornado segment because of my previous work. I haven't been able to get to a storm for the past two seasons." She fought to hold his gaze. She couldn't tell him that tornados had become monsters she feared instead of acts of nature she was in awe of. He would never agree if he knew she was scared.

"What makes you think you'll get one now?"

"Because you're with me." She hoped she didn't break down again while chasing, but if she did, he would be there for her. He would provide the shoulder to lean on unlike Austin. She didn't blame Austin. Even she didn't know what to do with herself, but having Cruz with her would bolster her confidence. At least he wouldn't leave her sobbing in a field.

"Things are different between us now."

"We might be breaking up for good, but you're still the same person who spent a career keeping people safe in combat. You know how to protect me, and I need that."

He narrowed his eyes and hesitated. She held her breath, waiting for him to back out or ask more questions about her wanting protection.

"Have you been watching the radar?"

She let go of that breath she held. "There's a system building with several storm possibilities in Kansas, near Colby. It's unusual this time of year, but a lucky break for July. I can't miss this last opportunity." Foster's text still rang in her mind. She had a week to produce or else.

"I might have noticed something on radar about

storms in Kansas. This would be a good time to try to intercept. I'm not saying I'm agreeing to this. Just making an observation."

"Then you watched the pattern too." She hoped her face remained neutral. She had to play this just right, not too much excitement, and not too much aloofness. There was a time she wouldn't have had to play Cruz at all. She would have climbed into his lap, straddled him, hooked her arms around his neck, and asked him.

"I've been busy with my new job. I only took a glance at the nationwide weather."

Two months ago he had started with the Brotherhood Protectors to provide air and terrain intelligence for their high-powered clients. She had been thrilled he left the military. He had risked his life too many times. At least now he would come home every night.

He had called to tell her that Mason, Ryder, and he were going as a team along with two other guys whose names she couldn't remember. She was glad to see Mason and Ryder had left too. Through everything, Cruz still kept her up to date with his life. She had taken that as a sign and supported his decisions without question, hoping it would bring him back to her.

"I could show you the radar. Of course, you can look yourself. I know you don't need me, but the cells are moving in the right direction. It could be something big by late this afternoon. My tracking skills aren't the best. Please, Cruz. I'll owe you."

He ran a hand over his face again. His fingers scratched at his beard. She liked that new adjustment too.

She waited. If she said anything first, he would say no, but all her arguments to his objections bubbled in her mouth like fizzy soda. She had to swallow them away.

"Why is the network worried about you? You didn't say."

"They're not actually worried. It's more like frustrated because I haven't accepted as many assignments."

"Why are you turning down assignments?"

If she told him, would he use it against her? She might if the tables were reversed. He would be in his right to hold her fear over her head.

"I don't want to be the camera person for the nightly weather report. And I don't want to go somewhere cold. They wanted to send me to see the penguins. I said no." That wasn't a complete lie. The network had asked her to take a camera operator spot on the evening news, but that had been a year ago and still during the time she thought she could beat the fear. Then the documentary with Foster came up so she grabbed on to it. Better than penguins, which was also a real offer she didn't want.

"Penguins?"

"It's cold there. And I would have to take a ship that can get through all the ice. Not my thing."

"I need a minute."

"I get it if you don't want to go. You don't owe me anything. I owe you. I'll owe you forever and now I'm putting another big ask in your lap."

She turned away and went into the kitchen, unable to bear the confused look in his eyes another second. If that look turned hurt or angry, she would fall apart. She was tired of disappointing him and plain old out of options if he said no. It would mean paying back her advance somehow and finding a new job in another field that didn't require references. She would have to find a way to make ends meet and finally move on from Cruz, let some other woman claim him.

She picked up the photo of them laughing over the white wedding cake with purple flowers. If she could go back in time, she would tell that young woman to give up chasing storms and natural disasters, to let someone else do it. Let someone else risk everything for a damn photo.

Cruz stood in the kitchen doorway with his hands on his hips. "Forty-eight hours. That's all I will give you. Then I'm gone."

"Thank you." She jumped into his arms and wrapped her legs around his waist like she had done a million times before, when they were a couple, a team, when he was her better half.

Only this time he didn't smile at her with his toothpaste commercial grin. She always envied him those white teeth. He narrowed his eyes and put her back on her feet.

"There will be one rule."

"Just one?" Sarcasm got the better of her. He always had specific ways of doing things. He wanted the bed made each morning. The covers had to be tight enough to flip a coin on them. He organized the pantry so all the labels faced out with like items on the shelves together. Towels were folded in thirds, and cardboard boxes were cut and flattened before placing them in the recycling bin.

"None of that jumping into my lap." He pointed between the two of them. "That's your space, and this is mine."

"Whatever you say, Lieutenant Colonel, sir." She mock saluted him. She hadn't thought about the leap before it happened. Excitement had sent her flying as if she stood on a springboard. He used to like it when she did that. It often led to making love. Even now, her body responded to his presence. Her breasts longed to press against his solid chest. Her most sensitive spot ached for his touch.

"Knock off that saluting stuff too. I'm plain old Cruz now. Just like in college." His words shook her dirty thoughts away.

"I don't know if I ever said this enough, but I've always been proud of you. You worked hard for what you have." She would watch him study in college, his nose in a book, his hand feverishly taking notes. He could sit in the library for hours, reading and absorbing all that scientific information that made her hair stand on end.

When he went into the Air Force, he put his discipline into training and constantly became better at whatever was asked of him. He could have been anything he wanted in this world. Ironically, he had been hers. And she had foolishly allowed him to go.

The crease between his brows softened. "Thanks. It's nice of you to say. You always worked hard too. You have determination in spades."

"Something that drove you crazy."

"Only sometimes." A small smile tugged at his lips.

"I guess we should go. I'd like to be near the storm area in a few hours. I packed snacks for the ride." She had purchased his favorites on the chance he would say yes. Part of her believed he always would. Cruz never let her down.

That had been her department.

WHAT HAD HE AGREED TO? He had walked straight into the black widow's spiderweb without so much as a hesitation. He had never liked her job of taking photographs of storms, especially the tornados. She risked her life each and every time. Part of her craved that adrenaline rush when she jumped back into the car and raced away from the edge of a tornado's madness and he didn't want to steal the challenge or the accomplishment, but he did want her to come home every time.

Seconds counted when she stood up to the tornado and snapped its picture without its consent. Tornados ate the things in its path without regard to person or place. Tornados were the monsters of the sky, and his wife tangled with them every year, along with every other natural disaster worth documenting.

The scar that ran down her arm from her shoulder to her elbow was the reminder of the time she had pushed the limits. The tattoo covered most of the scar now because she couldn't bear to see it every day. He couldn't either. As she had healed, the scar—a puckered red distortion on her smooth skin at first—tore his insides apart.

"We'll take my car, but you drive." She stowed her bag in the back seat of her little sedan, then tossed him the keys.

He grabbed his pack out of his truck, then hesitated by the driver's door. He wondered when she would tire of this work. "Ayla, are you sure you want to do this? I can loan you money, if you need it."

"Absolutely not. I won't take a loan from you. I have to do this. I have to prove to myself and everyone in the community I can get the big one."

"At what cost?"

"I don't know. What I do know is, I have to make this happen. I can't show up empty-handed to Foster. He will make sure I never work in this field again."

"Would that be so bad?" He had wanted her to see that it was time to do something else. Hell, part of the reason he left the Air Force was because it was a young man's game. He might be in good shape still, but he didn't bounce back from the miles of hiking and the hours of staying awake, fighting and planning, to make sure his teams were safe. He had to reinvent himself. Why couldn't she see that she could too?

"If I leave this field, I want to leave on my terms."

"You don't have anything to prove." They had this conversation many times. She drove herself as if something were on her back she couldn't shake. Whatever she attained she wanted more.

"That's easy for you to say. You've accomplished so much in your life, and you're only forty-one."

"You've done plenty."

"Really? I haven't won an award or had my work featured in any recognized exhibit or show for that matter. I've been working for a local news station, freelance work, the occasional indie documentary. But this assignment could change that for me."

"If you get the shots and the footage, will this be the end of storm chasing for you?"

"Why would you ask me that? I'm not thinking about next week or next month. All I'm thinking about is getting that perfect, mind-blowing shot. After that, I'll worry about what comes next." She blew her hair away from her face.

"We never get so close we can't get out. You have to listen to everything I say, even if it means you might not get the photo." He had to put parameters in place for their safety. He could not live with himself if anything happened to her that he could have avoided.

"You have to promise to get me as close as possible. You're going to have to let some of those rules of yours go. I have to come back with material that hasn't been seen before. Still shots and video." She climbed into the front seat and closed the door.

"It's dangerous. Promise me I have final say." He sat beside her and turned over the engine.

"I need the footage. You're going to have to take some risks. Please tell me you can do that."

"I won't take unnecessary chances. We can't control a tornado. Trying will only end up getting us killed. You have to respect the wind, Ayla." He had watched her defy the odds until her luck ran out. She pushed the boundaries too far sometimes. He wasn't ready to die today.

"But you know storms in a way no one else does. You don't need the instruments. You have your instincts, and they are never wrong."

"You're giving me a lot of credit." Credit he wasn't sure he wanted at the moment. He backed out of the driveway and turned onto the road. It looked as if he was going even if he continued to argue with her. He should quit the fighting. She could do what she wanted. She wasn't his problem.

"I need you. You'll keep me safe. If you had been with me that last time—"

"Don't. Don't go there. We don't talk about the last time at all on this trip. I won't be thrown off from what I need to do to bring you back in two days. You've played me enough just by getting me to agree to come along." The last thing he needed while trying to outrun a tornado was disconcerted thoughts about his past and his marriage. In order for them to return alive, he would have to be focused.

"I didn't want to manipulate you. I wasn't trying to play you, as you put it."

"Well, that's how it feels." She had wanted him

to talk about his feelings more, especially after they lost the baby, so here was his first attempt.

He weaved his way out of town and toward the interstate. He might feel played, but he still gave her exactly what she asked for. At least this trip, maybe he could control a few factors and return her home.

"I know how much you hate me. I needed a way to convince you to come here and listen to my plea."

"I don't hate you." His problem with her was worse. He may have never stopped loving her, this woman who refused to see her risks killed him every time she walked out the door.

"I always assumed your love for me had dried up and died that night. You could barely look at me for months afterward. You had walked out while I was on another assignment because you had been so disgusted."

"I really don't want to talk about this now." Images of Ayla jumping into his arms to tell him she was pregnant assaulted him.

He had returned home late from work at the base. The house had been dark and quiet. He figured she went to bed and hadn't waited up for him. He had become caught up in a project for a squadron about to take flight and lost track of the time.

"I'm up here," she had called from the bedroom. "Can you come up?"

He had climbed the stairs to find the hallway lit with candles on the floor, leading to their room. He had swallowed the wisecrack about the fire hazard she created and pushed the door open. She was by the window and turned to him. She took his breath away with the glow on her face and in her eyes when she saw him. He had hoped she would never stop looking at him like that.

The room was also filled with ivory candles. Their flames flickered and he had to stop himself from counting how many candles there were. Ayla had something planned. He should be grateful for that.

"What's going on?" he had said.

She ran across the room and jumped into his arms, almost knocking him over. "I have news."

"Sounds good. What kind of news?" He placed her on the bed and sat beside her, but she couldn't stay put and climbed into his lap, straddling him.

"I have something to show you." She stuck her hand in her pocket and pulled out a white stick.

"What's this?" The stick had two lines in a small window.

"I'm pregnant." She had squealed and kissed him hard on the mouth.

"Cruz, are you listening to me? I've been going on for a full minute and you zoned out," Ayla said.

He came crashing back into the small car with Ayla beside him in those wide-leg pants.

"What? Sorry. I was thinking about the road and the weather." And plenty of other things he had no business revisiting.

She rolled her eyes. He needed air and opened the window, but the humid breeze clobbered him as much as the memory.

"You have never wanted to talk about what happened. In the beginning it was too soon. Then you moved out and dodged me until I stood at your door and wouldn't go away. But even then you didn't want to talk about it. You wouldn't go to therapy with me. When is it supposed to be a good time to talk about the fact I lost our baby while chasing tornados?"

"Not hours before we're about to do that very thing." The pain had been unbearable in the beginning. Talking about it was like a gun exploding in his face. He thought time would have helped, but it hadn't.

The hikes had been the only thing to lessen the pain. For whatever crazy reason there was for hiking to be his salvation, it was. He didn't argue with the logic. For the first time ever, he didn't try to understand how something worked.

"Fine. We won't talk about it—again. We'll just do the job, and then you can go about your life, and

I won't bother you anymore either. This can be our last goodbye."

"Perfect."

"This will be strictly a business relationship. I will even pay you for your time, after I get paid."

He bit back a laugh and didn't remind her again that he paid her alimony even though the divorce wasn't final.

"I don't want your money." He truly did not. He didn't need it. The Brotherhood Protectors paid him well. He had some savings and half his pension which was decent since he'd been promoted before retirement.

"You deserve to be paid, and I will do that." She tilted up her chin. Her curls bounced off her shoulders.

"Fine. You can pay me an hourly rate. How's that?" He wouldn't take her money, but he would have a little fun, teasing her. She deserved it after the performance today. But she had been right about one thing. If she had told him on the phone what she wanted instead of in person, he would be hiking with his friends right now.

"Hourly? How about a flat fee for the two days?"

"I'm worth a lot. The Air Force said so. The Brotherhood does too." He flashed what he hoped was a cocky smile.

"I'm not one of those fancy princesses who needs your services because they're too wealthy to fly commercial and have to hire extra bodyguards. I need a reasonable quote."

"So, you do listen when I talk." When the new job had come through because he had known Hank Patterson and Jake Cogburn, he had called Ayla first. Out of habit. That was all that was. His call to her had nothing to do with the fact he always wanted to share his news with her before all others. Nothing.

"You come through loud and clear. Subtlety has never been your problem."

"Being direct stops confusion and saves lives."

"You know what? You're right. Let's not talk about us in any way. Just lay out the rest of your rules for this trip. I want to be prepared."

His attempt at humor fell flat. At least the thin line of her lips said so. The way back to her heart was closed off with yellow tape. No trespassing for him.

"Stay out of trouble. That's all I ask."

She mock saluted him again. "You got it, sir."

CHAPTER 4

SHE WAS a little harsh on him. He was trying to lighten the mood, but her nerves could choke an alligator. She had to keep her fears from Cruz. After she had the film she needed, then she could tell him her whole truth.

Ayla had let Cruz drive because she wanted to be able to hop out of the car to take pictures and videos, then hop back in before the tornado grabbed them and tossed them as if they weighed nothing. They cruised down Interstate 70, heading west toward Colby, Kansas, for the past two hours. The flatlands whizzed by on repeat. Scenery never changed in this part of the country. She preferred her space filled with trees that reached the sky and rolling hills or mountains.

Radar showed a cluster of possible storms in that region later this afternoon. They were roughly forty-five minutes from the location where the storms should form and hopefully turn into a tornado worth documenting.

Sitting so close to him ruined her focus. Instead of watching the radar on the laptop attached to her dashboard, her mind wandered to how he filled out the driver's seat with his long legs. Or how great he looked in his denim shirt and what was underneath that shirt. She hadn't had sex in over sixteen months, the time before she lost the baby, when her husband still loved her.

Her stomach churned with oily gasoline ready to explode inside her. She needed Cruz to bring the car close enough to the tornado, but with every mile under their belts, her skin grew tight and her breath shallow. What she did for a living was dangerous, but she couldn't stop herself any more than she could expect the sun to rise in the west. This must be what a smoker trying to quit felt like, always craving another drag that could be the end of them.

"Your car is a mess." He picked up a half-drunk bottle of Diet Coke that lost its fizz sometime last week from the cupholder.

Empty individual-size chip bags cluttered the floor and scattered greasy crumbs under her camera. Napkins were shoved in the open storage compartment in the door. She kept a grocery bag in the back seat filled with snacks and drinks.

Someone like her could be on the road for hours without a decent place to stop and get food. She didn't like to be without. She even kept rolls of toilet paper in the trunk.

"I don't clean it until chasing season is over. What's the point?"

"So it doesn't smell like a bologna sandwich."

"I don't eat that." A laugh fought its way out of her throat. Cruz smiled in her direction with a knowing glance that bologna was not in her food repertoire.

She didn't want to laugh. They were getting divorced. He shouldn't be funny any longer, but he was and always would be. Only in the future, some other woman would benefit from his humor.

Shifting in her seat, she pressed against the door. She needed some space from him and the feelings that remained like the lingering scent of floral perfume. Another woman will come along one day and take her place. This stranger will benefit from his sense of humor and quiet determination. Someone else will walk into his office late at night and find him bent over his computer, his eyebrows knit together as he solved a problem. Another woman will tap him on the shoulder and distract him from his work with a drop of her nightgown and a turn on her heel.

"Well, your car smells like you eat bologna and

mayo on white bread." He scrunched up his face as if in disgust, but he laughed at his own joke.

"I'll get an air freshener." She smiled back at him. It wasn't supposed to be easy to like him.

"Let's throw out some of the trash at the next gas station." He changed lanes.

"You're such a neat freak." But he was right. The car did have a rancid odor she had never noticed before. Sometimes that odor was her on the days her storm chasing covered her in mud and dust and kept her from a shower.

"Lucky for you."

"And lucky for you, I brought those spicy scoop-shaped corn chips you like so much." She reached behind the seat.

He arched a brow. "Seriously?"

"Do you want some?" She had to unhook her seat belt and climb between the seats. Her butt popped up in the air. She couldn't resist a peek in Cruz's direction. "Stop looking at my ass."

"I'm watching the road."

The crimson splash across his cheek said otherwise. She brought the bag into the front seat with her and attempted to contain her smile. "Do you want any?"

"Sure." He held out his hand.

She tore open the bag and plopped a spicy chip in his hand. Her fingers grazed his palm, and a lightning bolt shot through her arm to her chest. She yanked her hand away as if he had burned her.

Cruz narrowed his eyes. "You okay?"

"Great." Her voice came out high-pitched like some eighties rock singer screeching through a chorus.

He popped the chip in his mouth. "Can I have another?"

"Here. Take as many as you want." She placed the bag between his legs. Another mistake because her gaze landed right on his zipper.

Dust from the chips was on her fingers. She resisted the urge to lick it off and pulled out a napkin from the glove compartment instead.

"I like it better when you hand them to me."

"I'm not going to." She couldn't risk another shock like that.

"It's safer that way."

"Then I guess you don't need a snack." She took back the bag and shoved it on the floor. Not wanting to seem like an ungrateful bitch or a freak, she pushed her hair away from her face and tried a kinder conversation.

"I know I'm asking a lot of you on this trip. You're going to have to put us in harm's way. I appreciate what you're doing for me. I really do."

"We're going to stay safe. You can grab incredible photos away from the tornado's draft." He switched lanes again.

"The better shots will be up close, especially video. I need to know you're going to try to get near the funnel." So much for the kinder conversation. She couldn't control her emotions around this man.

"We won't be anywhere near its downdraft. I might be a meteorologist, but I'm not a storm chaser."

"Come on, Cruz. You're a damn retired combat weatherman. You mean to tell me that you can fight in a war, but you won't drive a few hundred yards away from a tornado moving in the opposite direction?"

He banged the steering wheel. "I took calculated risks. I knew as much information as I could about every mission before we went into it. Flying blind was not something I did, if I could help it, because lives were at stake. I did not want to call a mother and tell her that her son died under my command because I decided to throw caution away. Tornados aren't predictable, winds can change, air temperatures can change. Tornados hit one house and another, then miss the next one entirely. Don't compare what I did to what you do."

"You hate what I do."

When they first got married, she took photos of brides and grooms celebrating the innocence of a new marriage and elementary school children with holes in their mouths where teeth taken by the tooth fairy had been once. Cruz had encouraged her to keep going. He told her people needed her photos.

She had been bored with the predictability of gray backdrops and champagne flutes. She had thought about becoming a war correspondent for a hot second, but Cruz put an end to that right after his first tour when he came home shaken and different from the man he had been. The change had been subtle, but she knew him to his core and her Cruz was cracked in places that needed to be mended, but never were completely.

"Yes, I do. I hate it. I hate the storm chasing." He kept his gaze on the road. Storm clouds pressed down on them and rain began to fall in fat drops against the windshield.

"Then why are you here?" Her mood matched the dark, oppressive weather. Deep down she had been glad he objected to her idea of chasing destruction and death around the world. Part of her was afraid to stand in the line of fire to get the story. She hadn't been brave, at all. She never understood how Cruz could return to combat, but he had been determined to protect his country and all of those in it. It was no wonder he retired to become another kind of protector.

"Because I…"

"You what?" She would give just about anything to reach inside his stubborn mouth and pull out the words she hoped he would say. Maybe she was wrong, maybe Cruz didn't feel the way he used to about her, but a part of her still believed he loved her. He wouldn't say it because loving her meant getting hurt. Even she could figure that one out.

"Never mind. We're going to need to get gas soon. Do you want to fill up now before we get to Kansas? I can pull off the interstate here or we can wait a little longer."

"If we're near any towns, I'd like to film any destruction the tornado may cause. That kind of footage will be good for the documentary. People should see what a tornado can do. Maybe they'll listen to the warnings if they see its effect." Wanting to see a funnel cloud touch down churned elation and sorrow in her heart, two sides of a conflicted coin. She could make her career with the right footage, and innocent people might be hurt if the tornado tore through a town with no regard for anyone except its own selfish needs.

"I think the bigger problem is most tornado warnings end up being false alarms. People don't take the warnings seriously and don't seek shelter," Cruz said.

Weather had been a passion of hers, maybe because Cruz had also been her passion. After one too many bouquet tosses and father-daughter dances, an old professor had reached out to her. He had said the meteorology department was going to chase some storms and needed another photographer. Was she interested? She had been more than interested. Cruz had been overseas at the time. She was alone and bored and couldn't reach him to ask what he thought, so she went. And fell in love for the second time in her life.

"Get gas now or wait? Your call, Ayla."

"Let's try to go for a while longer. The weather is starting to turn." Dark, gray scud clouds hung low in the sky as if they might reach right down and touch the car with their jagged edges. An American flag, belonging to a tractor company that squatted to the side of the interstate, snapped in the wind that would be cool and moist right now if she stuck her hand out the window to test. This summer day's warm air waited for that wind like a chef waiting on the delivery of perfect ingredients. Without that flawless recipe of cool wind and warm air, no thunderstorm could form and build into a tornado.

She wouldn't be so lucky to have a tornado form right away so they could end this trip as quickly as it started. Her fears continued to crawl out of her belly and threatened to take hold. She needed to think about something besides tornados.

"I'm thinking about selling the house." She hadn't planned on telling him that just yet, but planning had never been her strong suit.

Cruz's gaze flashed in her direction before returning to the road. "Why?"

"I can't really afford to keep it, and I'm hardly ever there. It makes sense to downsize. Maybe get a condo." She fidgeted with the buttons on the camera to give her something to look at besides him.

She hadn't wanted to sell the house, but walking around the rooms that echoed without him in them had become too much to bear. That was why she was rarely there—that and the unused nursery.

"That's probably a good idea. You won't have to worry about flooding basements any longer either." He turned on the wipers, and their blades swooshed against the windshield and cleared a clean view forward.

"You aren't sorry to see the house go?" She had wanted him to protest even a little to show her he might still care in some way. He had retreated into himself after her accident and she did not know how to wrap her fingers around him and bring him back. She waited for a sign, any kind of sign, on how to return him to her, but there were none.

"It's just a house." And more signs that he had moved on without her.

"We built a life there." They had picked out drapes and carpet and rearranged furniture. They had to take the molding off their bedroom door to get their mattress in the room. They had painted the kitchen and family room themselves, getting more paint on each other than the walls. They had shared coffee in the mornings and made love in the afternoons and evenings in every room of the house.

"It's time to build a life somewhere else."

She opened her mouth to ask what he meant by that, as if she didn't know, but the cloud formation changed. Just a few miles ahead the scud had condensed and rose, organizing into a wall cloud. There was a good chance a tornado could occur. She checked the radar. Areas of red outshone those of yellow, orange, and green. The pixelized shape moved rapidly over her screen.

"Cruz, we're west of that thunderhead. We need to get off the interstate."

"It's not a tornado."

"Those are wall clouds—why am I telling you? You know what you're looking at." She rolled down the window. Raindrops flew in, but she ignored them and pointed her camera toward the massive shelf of clouds. Wind blew her hair against her cheek. She brushed it off.

They were too far away for any great shots, but some of the footage might be useful for the documentary. She would know better when she could sit comfortably in her home and play back whatever was recorded.

"Okay, if you insist. It's your rodeo." Cruz sat

forward in the seat and took the exit for the local road. His fingers gripped the wheel until his knuckles turned white.

The landscape, what little there was besides open fields, flew by. The car pushed against the wind, and it pushed back. Clouds hurried away like evil children with hollowed eyes and unwashed hair that taunted their pursuers. But the storm, heavy with unshed precipitation, was no match for Cruz as he continued to race ahead. The distance between them and the pending storm shrunk.

Her fears grew spindly legs with fur and scaled from her belly to her throat until her mouth was full of panic and worry. She clamped her lips shut to keep the scream from escaping. Cruz couldn't find out the panic had begun. He would pull over immediately, or worse turn around, and she needed the shots, even just one.

Sweat broke out over her body. Her vision narrowed until the storm clouds were nothing more than a dot of gray surrounded by black. Every raindrop blurred that vision further. All she wanted was to get out of the car and run in the other direction as fast as she could, but she forced her hand to stay away from the door handle.

She positioned the camera for a shot, but her hands shook. Her fingers failed to follow the commands to hold on tightly and dropped the camera which knocked her knee and hit the floor with a thud.

Cruz said something, but he was a million miles away, and she couldn't hear him even if his mouth moved. His eyes grew as wide as the shelf cloud in front of them. He gripped her shoulder, the pressure running down her arm, but she was helpless to answer him back. The panic picked up speed like the rain and the wipers. Frantic thoughts played as if an out-of-control orchestra with no conductor carried on in her head.

He jerked the car to a stop on the side of the road, and she lunged forward in the seat. Her seat belt shoved her backward, knocking the back of her head on the headrest.

"Are you okay?" Cruz turned to her.

"I'm good." She was anything but okay, needing to put her head between her knees to make the world stop spinning, but there wasn't enough room. If she stuck to her story, maybe they would both believe it.

"You don't look so good."

"I'm okay. Just go after that tornado." The words held a frenetic quality as if she could no longer control her vocal cords. But everything was urgent when a storm was involved. People hurried for safety. Animals bucked, cawed, and barked. Chasers intercepted danger.

"Tell me what's going on. Your face is gray. You look like you might puke."

"I'm fine. Why won't you believe me? Don't you understand how important this is to me?"

"Ayla, stop yelling and tell me what is going on."

Was she yelling? The interior of the car pushed in on her. She jumped out. Rain pelted her, soaking her white tank top. In seconds, Cruz would be able to see right through it, but her modesty didn't matter. What mattered was her career. She gulped in wet air as the clouds a few miles up ahead dropped a funnel that may have touched down, destroying everything in its path. The tornado moved in the opposite direction, as if to jeer at them and taunt that it could never be caught.

Cruz hurried to her. Rain soaked him too, but he didn't seem to notice. He gripped her shoulders, forcing her to look at him.

"Why are we standing out here in the rain? Tell me, or I'll throw the car keys into the field and we'll never get to that tornado. Tell me." Fear flashed in his eyes or it was the reflection of her own. She didn't want to scare him too and needed to calm down before he did exactly what he threatened.

"I'm sick. I have a stomach bug. I didn't want to tell you." She forced her gaze to stay on his. She hated lying to him. He deserved better than that, but she couldn't admit what was really going on with her, at least not yet.

Every time she had tried to run into a storm, panic took hold with two big hands and froze her in her spot. Her body didn't respond to the orders her brain screamed. Her arms and legs became limp. Sweat soaked her until she reeked. Her heart pounded until she was certain its only option was to bust free of her ribs.

He released his grip and stepped back, wiping rain off his face. "You didn't want to throw up in the car. I get it now. Do you feel better? Are you ready to get back on the road?"

He didn't question her excuse and that added to the guilt. He also hadn't noticed any of her other strange behavior which meant she could probably keep up this charade for a while longer.

"I feel a little better. The fresh air and even the rain helped." She slid into the car without looking at him. Her wide-leg pants dripped onto the floor. She shivered against the air conditioning that blew out of the vents and pushed their direction away from her.

The back door swung open and Cruz rummaged through the bag of snacks and drinks she had brought, pulling out a diet soda.

"Here. Sip this." He handed it to her between the seats.

She opened her mouth to protest, but she almost gagged instead. Admitting defeat, she twisted open the cap and drank.

He slid back in beside her and ran a hand through his wet hair, looking incredible even rain logged. "Are you sure it's only a bug? You seemed fine this morning."

"It comes, and it goes." Hopefully, it was gone for good, but she knew better. The severe weather didn't have to be a tornado. It could be a tropical storm or a heavy snowfall. Whenever the weather turned bad, her insides turned to a gloppy mess.

His gaze searched her face as if he were trying to determine whether she had told the whole story or any of it. He knew her too well, all their years together. She could never hide what she was feeling from him. She had been an open book, but she hoped these last months apart would be in her favor.

"Okay, but tell me if you need me to stop. I can always take a photo or two if you're sick."

She stifled a groan. She was lying to him and he was being kind to her.

"Sure. Thank you."

Cruz pulled back onto the interstate and raced to the storm's location. She didn't say anything as the miles shortened, but gripped the seat with both hands.

Wind continued to assault the car, and the sky morphed as the road dipped south. The clouds shifted. The funnel disappeared as if the wall clouds sucked it back inside their massive formation.

"It's gone," Cruz said.

"Let's see if it touched down."

Cruz took the exit and made turns as if he had driven these roads often. He hadn't, but his sense of direction was as incredible as his instincts for weather. She would get lost in a bag and may have once or twice.

A blue and gold sign on the side of the road informed them they were welcome in Sugar, Kansas, population 3,004. The rain had stopped and spots of blue sky poked through the clouds as a reminder of better times.

"I don't know this town. Do you?" Cruz said.

"I don't think so."

Trees lined the road on both sides. Branches and leaves littered the road and Cruz had to avoid hitting a few larger branches strewn across the pavement. Maybe there hadn't been much destruction from this storm.

The trees gave way to open space, and her mouth dropped. Destruction met them on one side of the road. A tornado had swooped down and ate everything in its path, leaving the other side of the road untouched. A large oil tank sat unscathed where the damage had been done, but everything else was rubble. Cars were upside and crushed like a tin can. An auto shop was gone, but the gas tanks remained. Lucky, considering a massive explosion could have happened if those tanks had been ripped out of the ground.

"Cruz, my God." She gripped his arm.

"I know. I don't see anyone. Hopefully, they all got to safety."

"All of them?" The probability of that was low. Sometimes people didn't hear the warning or worse—ignored it. "Should we stop and look?"

"Definitely. It doesn't look like any first responders are here yet." He pulled over by a coffee shop that had been spared as had its neighbors, an art gallery and a small clothing boutique. Those buildings had a front row seat to the devastation.

Cruz hopped out and looked through the window of the café. "No one is in there. That's a good sign. Let's see if we can find anyone."

They picked through the rubble, careful of where they stepped, calling out, but no one answered. She didn't know how it could be possible, but maybe the whole town had taken shelter.

"Is anyone here?" Cruz cupped his hands around his mouth and yelled.

They walked down the street a little, still approaching what must have been businesses and a few small houses sprinkled in between. They were the only souls on the road as if this town dropped out of the sky with the tornado and no one actually lived here.

A sign reading Dolly's Day Care in faded pink letters stood sentry to the broken glass and shredded roof of what must have been Dolly's. Ayla's breath caught.

"Cruz, a day care. What if there are children in there?" She couldn't bear to look but had to find out.

"Come on." He took her hand, and she let him because she could not face what might wait for them without his help.

Two walls of the day care still stood. The big bad tornado had huffed and puffed but couldn't knock down the brick. They stepped over beams and pushed aside fallen cubbies. Small desk chairs in red and blue lay on their sides. Crayons and markers scattered over the mess like toxic confetti.

"Is anyone here?" Cruz called out.

She picked up a child's jacket covered in dust and fisted the material. Panic fluttered in her belly. She swallowed the desire to scream. Being in this place, where children were supposed to be safe, filling their days with laughing and learning, tormented her. Children were not supposed to be hurt. A parent wasn't supposed to outlive her child. A child being taken first was the wrong order of things. Something her brain could not comprehend no matter how long time continued to turn. Her child should have been born. She would have gladly given her life if it had meant her baby could have lived a full life with his daddy.

"No one is here, Ayla. They must've evacuated." Cruz freed the jacket from her grip and placed it to the side.

"Are you sure?"

"People would be yelling for help."

"But behind that wall, where does it lead?" One of the interior walls also still stood. A miracle, but Ayla had witnessed homes ravaged by tornados where from the street the home appeared untouched, every tree upright, even the welcome mat in place. But inside the front door, the back of the house had been sliced away as if a giant had used a jagged knife to cut through the wood beams and drywall. A kitchen and family room once securely in place had disappeared as if that giant was also an evil magician who made things vanish.

"I'll check. Stay here," he said.

"I want to go with you." Broken windows in the remaining walls pulsed with her own rapid heartbeat. She didn't want to stand amongst the ruin, waiting for the windows to explode on her.

"I think you should stay put. We don't know what's in there."

"I'm coming." She gripped his hand. He shook his head, but he didn't let go.

They passed through a swinging door that opened into a small kitchen without windows, but with a sink, a couple of cabinets, and a square wood table for four. One plate with a half-finished snack of apples and peanut butter was left on the table. A standup shelf tower had fallen on its side, blocking what might be a pantry.

"Did you hear that?" She turned in the direction of a muffled response.

"I didn't hear anything."

"Hello? Does anyone need help?"

"Help. I'm stuck in here." Pounding accompanied the muffled voice coming from the pantry. "Please hurry," the female voice said and then groaned.

"She must be hurt," Cruz said to her and then to the door, "we're coming. Ayla, call 911 just to make sure someone knows to come out here. I'll move the shelf."

Cruz strained against the wood that was taller than he was, but her strong man heaved until the shelf stood upright. She told the 911 operator what was happening and to hurry with help. Whatever police and fire this town of Sugar had might be all tied up helping others, if they could even get out from wherever they were.

Cruz pulled open the door to what was, in fact, a pantry with floor-to-ceiling shelves. Every shelf was filled with crackers, popcorn, juice boxes, cake mix, and every paper product possible from tissues to tampons.

A woman sat on the floor, leaned against the back shelves, and held her stomach. Her chest heaved with every breath. Her skin glistened with sweat, her hair plastered to her forehead. She gnawed on her bottom lip as she looked at them. A puddle of water covered the floor in front of her.

"Oh, shit," Cruz said.

"My thoughts too. I'm having a baby. Right now."

CHAPTER 5

CRUZ HAD NEVER DELIVERED a baby before. From the looks of this young woman, groaning every other minute, this baby might be coming and they wouldn't have time to get her to the hospital. If the hospital was still standing, anywhere near where they were, and not inundated with other people hurt in the storm.

The mother-to-be—in about a minute—had an oval face with a pointy chin. She couldn't be more than twenty-five. Her blond hair hung in strings around her sweaty face. Her brown eyes were glassy and wide as if she hadn't considered the baby might come out—ever. The pantry smelled of body odor.

"How long until the police or fire department arrive?" He turned to Ayla. Her mouth hung open. She stood frozen in place. Seeing a woman give birth could be overwhelming, but her face resembled terror.

"Ayla." He snapped his fingers. "What did the 911 operator say?"

She jumped. "What? Oh. She didn't know how long. Calls are coming in everywhere."

"Ma'am, my name is Cruz Lacerda and this is my wife Ayla. Are you hurt?"

"Besides this baby ripping me in two?" The woman sucked in air.

"I'll take that as a no. We're going to try and help you." His military training taught him to assess the problem and come up with an innovative way to handle it when the typical way was unavailable. The conventional way to deliver a baby was definitely not accessible to him.

"Well, you'd better start helping because this baby is coming. Ooooh." She gripped her belly and bent in half.

"What do we do?" Ayla looked between him and the woman.

"Ma'am, what is your name?"

"Aaahh. It's Erin."

"Okay, Erin. I have some medical training; we're going to get through this just fine until help comes." He took off his denim shirt and put it to the side. They might need it for the baby.

The town water supply could be shut down. Power would be out. And the structure of what was left of this building was compromised. They needed to get out of the pantry.

"Ayla, I need a clear path to the car. Can you do that?"

"Sure." She ran off.

"Can you walk?" he said to Erin.

"I don't know." She stared at him with wide eyes.

"You lean on me, and I'll get you outside and away from the building." He helped Erin stand.

She came up to his chin. Erin was taller than Ayla and built differently. Ayla never got to be this pregnant. He would have liked to see what she had looked like with his baby inside her and ready to come out. She would have been beautiful.

"I don't want to have my baby in a car." She pressed her weight against him.

"You don't want to have it in a pantry." He guided her into the kitchen.

Erin bent forward in a rush and almost right out of his hold. She screamed. "This baby is coming now. I have to push. I can't wait. We have to do it here."

Ayla ran through the door and back into the room. "Okay. I think we can make it to the car."

"Forget the car. We're doing this now. Help me get Erin on the table."

"Now?"

"Yeah, babe. We're going to deliver a baby."

Aʏʟᴀ ᴅɪᴅ ɴᴏᴛ ᴡᴀɴᴛ to deliver a baby. She didn't know how, had never seen one born. Both of her brothers had kids, but she had sat safe in the waiting room and away from babies coming into the world. She had never wanted to see a baby being born and after her accident, she didn't even want to see pregnant women.

"I can't." She took a step back.

Cruz arched a brow. "I need you to push the table against the cabinets so Erin can lean against something."

She didn't move. "Cruz... I..."

"Hang on to Erin. I'll move the table." He waved her over. When she didn't move again, his long reach took her by the wrist and gently tugged her. "You can do this." He stepped away.

Erin dropped into her like a heavy bag coming loose from its hook. She gripped Erin around the waist and kept her standing by some miracle. The smell of sweat and peanut butter emitted off this woman.

"Thank you for catching me," Erin said between deep breaths.

"Sure thing." Her stomach turned in on itself and bile burned her throat. She could not panic now. This woman needed their help. Cruz needed her to be strong and not fall apart, but her knees still tried to give up. She locked them into place.

"Help me get Erin on the table." Cruz came around the other side of Erin and together, the three of them seated Erin on the table with her back against the counter.

Another contraction came and Erin screamed like a lead singer in a heavy metal band. Ayla helped Erin get her bottoms off.

Cruz remained calm, offering soothing words as Erin gripped the side of the table, gritted her teeth, and yelled.

"I need to push."

"On the next contraction, give it a shot." Cruz turned to her. "Babe, grab my shirt out of the pantry. We're going to need it. Also, see if there are any dish towels in the drawers, okay?"

Erin let out a holler that must have come from her toes.

"You're doing great. Take a breath. On the next one, push with all you have."

Ayla didn't understand how Cruz knew what he was doing. He had all kinds of intense training, but she was pretty sure no one had delivered any babies on the battlefields. She pulled open drawers, but didn't find anything of use.

Erin yelled again, and her eyes rolled back in her head. Sweat soaked the top of her shirt. Her chest heaved and Ayla hoped Erin was getting enough oxygen. They should be in a hospital with experts, people trained to take care of mothers and their babies.

She tried not to think about the morose faces of the doctors and nurses when they told her that they had done all they could, but the baby was lost anyway. She had come to in the hospital room. Her arm was bandaged, and she was hooked up to several machines that beeped and burped out information about her vitals.

Cruz had stood in the corner of the room while the male doctor with a bald head and wireless glasses explained what had happened. She had only heard accident and lost the baby. Everything else the man had said hadn't computed. She had reached a hand out for Cruz. He had taken her hand, but in that moment, something was different between them.

"Babe, you still with me?" Cruz's words dumped her back into the half-standing day care where she was supposed to be looking for something.

"Right here."

"Did you find the dish towels?"

Dish towels. That was what she needed.

"Nothing. Sorry."

If something went wrong with Erin and the baby, would Cruz know what to do? She couldn't watch another woman lose her child. She wanted to wait for the ambulance, but that was an unreasonable request. This baby was on its way whether the rest of the world was ready or not.

"That's okay." He turned to Erin. "You're almost there. I think I can see a head. Next contraction, push hard," Cruz said.

"I can't." Erin shook her head.

"You've got to. Your baby wants to meet you." Cruz gave Erin's hand a squeeze.

Tears choked her. Cruz always knew the right thing to say. When they lost their baby, he had shut down from the grief. Everything he said to her had come out wrong. At least, that was how she heard it. She should have stayed around to help him, work things through with him, instead of going back to chasing storms. The answers hadn't been out there.

"Aaahh." Erin pushed into a seated position and grunted. She flopped back down.

"That counter must be uncomfortable. I'll be right back." She needed air.

"Ayla, I need you to stay here," Cruz said.

"I have a blanket in the car." She ran out of the building before Cruz could say anything else. She wanted to help Erin, but she needed to get away from the smell of body odor and possible death.

In all the months since she lost the person she loved most—and she had loved that little baby swimming inside her even though they hadn't met —she fought against the sadness, anger, and frustration of an unfair life. Some days only one of those emotions took control. Other days she was helpless to all of them.

In order to survive, she had to crawl back to something that resembled joy. At first, it was seeing a friend for lunch. From there it grew to using her camera again, and then back to chasing storms because that was the only thing left that brought her any joy at all. When she had left to chase right after the baby had died, she wasn't following her joy. She was running from terror.

Outside the day care, she jumped over fallen debris, hoping she didn't land wrong and twist an ankle. Her blanket was in the back of the car for those unexpected overnight stops or sleeping in her car, which she had done on more than one occasion.

The streets remained empty except for the broken buildings. Other than the grizzly cry of the wind, nothing spoke back. No birds sang nor voices carried. She strained to find even the smallest whoosh of a passing car nearby, but only silence answered her.

A sinister sliver slipped down her spine. She tried to shake it off. This town was wrong. Bad things had happened here before today. She never wanted to return to Sugar, Kansas. Reaching the car, she grabbed the blanket and hurried back.

"Here." She placed the blanket behind Erin.

"Thank you. That's much better." Erin's lips were cracked and her breath smelled like stale coffee. The poor woman was probably dehydrated.

Ayla checked the freezer section of the refrigerator and found ice. She crushed some with the handle of a large knife and pressed some to Erin's lips.

"Oh, that's so nice. Thank you both for helping me." A tear ran down Erin's face.

"Get ready, Erin," Cruz said. He was sweating now and wiped his brow with the hem of his t-shirt.

Erin let out another high-pitched screech. Her face bloomed beet red. The veins in her temples bulged.

"Ayla, get behind Erin and help her sit up." Cruz pushed up Erin's leg at the knee.

She positioned herself behind Erin's hot, wet body, giving her something to push against. Erin bore down again. Ayla gritted her teeth too as if her grunting could help and almost laughed at herself.

"Here comes the top of the head." Cruz's smile burst wide. "Give me one more."

Erin grunted and pushed.

"The head is out." Tears filled Cruz's eyes.

Tears stung her eyes too. She peered over Erin's shoulder. A tiny head poked free.

"Cruz, oh my God." A warm flush ran over her. She couldn't believe what was happening.

"I know, babe." His gaze caught hers, and he looked right into her soul. His look said what she was thinking. This was supposed to be them.

"Is he okay?" Erin strained to see.

Cruz's gaze snapped away and the connection was broken or she imagined it.

"Your baby is fine. One more push, and we should be able to get out a shoulder."

A few pushes later, a beautiful baby boy slid into Cruz's outstretched arms. He wrapped the baby in his denim shirt. The three of them laughed and cried. Cruz handed the baby to a very worn out but smiling mother.

"Thank you. I couldn't have done that myself." Erin kept her gaze on her baby.

"I'm guessing you were here alone?" Cruz said.

"The day care closed this morning. The weather reports were saying signs of bad weather, but I came in to take care of some bills. I stopped for a snack and the next thing I knew, the building shook on its foundation. I thought the room was going to tumble end over end. I jumped into the pantry. The shelf fell in front of the door, and I was stuck. Thank God the two of you came by."

"Do you own the place? The sign out front says this is Dolly's Day Care," she said.

"Dolly was my aunt. She moved to Arizona a year ago. I took over." Erin shifted and winced. The baby looked up at his momma. His eyelashes were long enough to touch his eyebrows.

"Do you have someone to call?" Cruz pulled his phone out of his back pocket. "I'm not sure how cell service is, but I can try."

"My boyfriend Al. He works around the corner at the insurance agency. Do you know if the tornado went that way?"

She took Erin's hand. "We'll find out."

Erin gave Cruz her boyfriend's number. He stepped away to call, claiming he might get better service on the street. But she had to wonder if it had more to do with keeping the news from Erin if he stumbled upon something bad.

"Could you get more ice cubes? That was heavenly."

Ayla put some ice chips in a cup this time and held it out. Erin looked between her and the baby. "Would you like to hold him?"

She took a step back and hit the counter. "Oh, I don't think I had better. He looks so comfortable. I wouldn't want to disturb him." She didn't wait for Erin to say anything and popped an ice chip in the woman's mouth.

"Do you two have children?" Erin said around the ice.

"No."

"Maybe someday then."

"We're getting a divorce." She didn't know why

she had said that. What would it matter to this woman they would never see again if they were married and in love or married and waiting for the day the judge said otherwise? It would matter not at all. Her relationship with Cruz mattered to her alone.

"Really? I wouldn't have guessed by the way he looks at you."

"Like I have two heads?"

"Like he wants to kiss the hell out of you. I wish Al looked at me like that. He loves me. Don't get me wrong. He's a good guy and will make a great father, but passion isn't exactly his strong suit."

Cruz had always been a typical guy's guy and she loved that about him. But when it was just the two of them, especially in bed, he let go and showed her how deep his emotions ran. He could be very passionate in the old days. She wouldn't have been able to marry him if he wasn't like that with her. But she didn't want to judge Erin and her boyfriend. Erin might just have the life Ayla had dreamed of for herself.

Cruz returned with a man dressed in fire gear. "Good news. I reached Al. He's okay and on his way here. And I found Lieutenant Perry here. He's going to help you and the baby."

"Howdy. The stretcher is on its way." Lieutenant Perry tipped his fire hat.

"Hey, did you have a name picked out? I'd love

to hear it before they take you two to the hospital," Cruz said.

"We were thinking about naming him Alexander, after his daddy. Al didn't want that. He said it would be too confusing for them both to have the same name." Erin looked down at her baby again. Her eyes filled with love. "I'm thinking his name should be Cruz Alexander. Then he will have the first name of the man who delivered him and his middle name will start with an A for Ayla too."

Her body flushed with heat again. Cruz put an arm around her shoulders and pulled her against him. "How about that, babe? A baby named after us." He beamed at her.

And she burst into tears.

CHAPTER 6

Cruz PULLED BACK onto the interstate. Night had crept in while they were helping some of the first responders look for survivors. When Lieutenant Perry had learned that Cruz was former military with combat training, he had recruited him for some of the search and rescue. Cruz had been more than happy to help. She had assisted too. Cruz always kept her close by, but after an hour, she needed a break and returned to the car. Several people were injured. No one had died and one baby was born.

"Are you okay?" he said.

"I'm ready to get out of this town. I don't like it here." She looked out the passenger window at the death and destruction left behind. People would have to spend months rebuilding their lives. Some wouldn't be able to rebuild at all.

"Even after we delivered a baby?" He stole a glance at her.

"It was amazing and sad at the same time. But the quietness of the street where we were. Why wasn't anyone there?" Ayla's body tingled with the excitement of bringing a new baby into the world and vibrated with the pain of what she lost.

"I don't know. Maybe not too many people live there. Or they all found shelter elsewhere. Lieutenant Perry said the high school was used as a shelter. Most people were there."

"I'm glad to be leaving."

Cruz gripped her knee and gave it a squeeze. "I'll find us a place to spend the night. We're near a small town named Radiant."

"How do you know that?" She shifted to get a better look at him. New hair growth dotted the line above his very close beard. He never had facial hair while he was in the Air Force. She had no idea she even found a beard sexy until Cruz wore it like a champ. No other man came close to him.

"Mason, Ryder, and I stayed at a cattle ranch during college. We wrangled cattle." He flashed his silly smile at her. The one he used to get an extra laugh out of her.

"Of course, you three did. And Mason probably hated every minute of it. I had forgotten that dumb guy's trip." That might have been the only other time Cruz had grown a beard. Had she liked it then too? When he came back from the trip, she would have jumped his bones—beard or not.

"It was my idea. I think it fit with a science class I had to take. You certainly weren't going to come with me." He took right and left turns as if he'd been in this part of the state a hundred times.

"Heck, no. Cattle and mud is more your thing."

They followed the road until they came to town. Her stomach growled. She hadn't eaten all day and with night upon them, she could sink her teeth into a juicy burger.

"There must be some kind of diner nearby and open late. I hope, anyway," Cruz said.

Radiant was anything but. The main road sliced through town like a rusted knife. Old buildings and tired houses stared back at them. Radiant and Sugar had a lot in common, and she didn't like it. Very little light spilled down from the streetlamps and lit windows to illuminate the street and push the darkness into corners.

A single traffic light swayed in the wind. Tumbleweeds crossed the street in front of them. A square-shaped house with clapboards that looked gray, but might have once been a happy white, was obscured by an overgrown pear tree. Someone had abandoned a bicycle on the front lawn. Its wheel spun as if the rider had recently tossed it down, but the patchy yard was empty.

A few boarded-up stores with scarred paint

dotted the scenery on either side of the road, a reminder that Radiant may have been a place where nice people raised their children or came to visit Grandma on Sundays or where a woman could find the latest fashion at Martha Rae's dress shop that had one floral dress in the window—something Ayla would never wear. She could imagine, though, an older Radiant where the sidewalks were filled with residents, tipping their hats to their neighbors, stores burst with customers, and picnics were a regular occurrence.

At the next corner was a bank, still in use, if the advertisement for low interest rate mortgages in the window was any indicator. The year 1883 faded into the white brick at the top of the building. The post office—definitely closed—all the windows were dark as it was after hours, sat beside the police station. At the end of the road that broke off in different directions was exactly what Ayla's stomach longed for—Max's Hash House.

Behind Max's Hash House was Max's Motel. The two places shared the same parking lot. Max's Motel was a squat two-story building with ten light-gray doors on each floor that faced the parking lot. The vacancy sign blinked in a frenzy of red and green as if it wasn't sure whether the rooms were vacant or not. Her body ached from head to toe. Max's Motel would do just fine. She wouldn't look too closely for dirt or DNA.

Cruz parked in front of the motel office. "We can grab dinner and stay at the motel."

She stretched with a yawn. "I could probably go right to bed."

"I'll get us separate rooms." He hopped out of the car as if someone just lit his butt on fire.

She hadn't meant the words the way they may have sounded, but she doubted he would believe her after her big come-on earlier today. She hadn't thought about what she was saying, actually. She only wanted something to eat and a good night's sleep. If he needed to stay away from her, she would find a way to understand. Sharing the experience of watching a life come into the world should have bonded them. It hadn't.

She pushed out of the car. "Why don't you go get us rooms, and I'll order some food. Is that okay, Lieutenant Colonel?"

"What did I say now?" He scratched his fingers against his beard.

"What makes you think you said anything?" It wasn't what he said, it was how fast he jumped out of the car that said it all.

"The only time you use my rank is when you think I'm trying to control everything."

"Aren't you?" She couldn't remember a time when Cruz didn't try to control something from the way the coffee maker should be on the counter to the direction of the toilet paper.

"Why? Because I want us to have separate rooms to sleep in? I suggested that because I figured it was what you wanted."

"You walked out on me." She wasn't talking about the car anymore.

"No, you walked out on me. I left after you made your choice."

She looked at the ground before returning her gaze to him. He was right, but she wouldn't say it. She had been afraid, just like she was twice today. Cruz wasn't afraid of anything. He looked fear in the eye all the time and told it to screw off. He was the bravest person she had ever known.

"I'll get us hamburgers." She turned to walk inside, and he grabbed her wrist.

"Hey, let's not fight, okay? We did something incredible today. Tomorrow we'll find your storm, and you'll do something else incredible. The past doesn't matter tonight."

It all still mattered to her. Every bit of it. And maybe some of it mattered to him too, but her mouth wouldn't ask the questions in case she was wrong. She couldn't handle the rejection with her nerves so raw from the day.

And worse, what if her question led to an answer that involved another woman? If he told her that he had moved on, she would fall apart, probably beg him to take her back. Did she want to beg? No, he had left her. She would not beg.

But if there was another woman, Cruz would not leave this person—made up or otherwise—and stay with her. He would not break up with someone because something better had come along. If he made a commitment, he stuck with it. Someone else had to cut ties first.

"No fighting. No past. Just burgers." She could pretend for a little while longer that she was over him. She had to get through the next day. He had promised her forty-eight hours only. After that, she could ask him the hard questions. Maybe he'd even answer them.

"I'll meet you inside." He headed for the corner of the motel where the office window was lit and a large woman, looking at her phone, sat inside behind a counter. Ayla turned for the Hash House.

Max's Hash House smelled like grease. Her shoes stuck to the floor with each step. The place was mostly empty this time of night. A typical dinner hour had passed. She hoped some of the residents were preparing for any foul weather coming their way and that was keeping them out of Max's Hash House.

"Grab a menu and seat yourself," A heavyset man with loose hanging jowls and a scraggly beard said from behind the counter. That was a beard that needed a little personal time with a good trimmer. He tossed a towel over his shoulder and pushed through the swinging doors to the kitchen.

She took the booth toward the back by the window and faced the door. Cruz would be able to find her when he arrived. She perused the menu, but nothing looked good. Her stomach might want food, but her mind raced backward to all the hurt feelings between her and Cruz, places she didn't want to visit on any day.

The last time she had left to chase, he had asked her not to go.

"I don't want anything to happen to you," he had said.

Nothing had happened to her before. "I'll be fine."

"But you're going alone."

"I'll stay back. I just need to get some new shots. A couple of places are interested in buying them." She had planned to stay out of the way, but she couldn't put a lid on her excitement once the storm formed. Then one wrong turn had cost her more than she had wanted to pay.

Cruz slid in the booth opposite her, startling her. She tossed the menu on the table.

"There's good news and bad news. Which do you want first?" He grabbed the menu and browsed it.

"Let's get the bad news over with. Like pulling a tooth."

He flattened the menu on the table. "We have to

share a room and a bed unless one of us sleeps on the floor."

Sharing a bed sounded like good news to her. She stifled the smile that pulled on her lips.

"What's the good news?"

"They had a room. And the floor looks clean." He pressed his lips together in a thin smile.

"I'm not sleeping on the floor." She could pretend to be an independent woman who didn't need a man to be uncomfortable for her, but she didn't want to sleep on the floor. She had enough bad nights' sleep to last her. She would share the bed, though.

"I'll take the floor."

"You don't have to do that."

"I do."

She looked out the window, but her reflection stared back. Her curls stood up in the back. She ran a hand through her hair, trying to smooth them to no avail. Her skin sagged under her eyes and around her jaw. If someone saw her, they would think she hadn't slept in months. She would tell them she hadn't slept in sixteen months.

"What are you going to order?"

She turned at the female voice filled with bouncing gravel. The waitress, with her order pad in her hand, cleared her throat and stared at Ayla. The woman's hair was pulled back in a greasy ponytail. Her roots were black and white, but the hair hanging in the tail was a brassy blond. Her black collared shirt was covered in stains that Ayla didn't want to know what their origin might be.

"We'll have the burgers and unsweetened iced tea." Cruz handed the waitress the menus.

"How do you want them cooked?" Ponytail scratched her pen against the paper.

"I'll take mine medium. Ayla?"

"I don't care." She crumpled a napkin in her fist.

She slid out of the booth and headed for the door. The air in the diner thickened, making it hard for her to breathe. The diner's cloying smell and the cracked capillaries across the waitress' nose and under her eyes turned Ayla's stomach.

Cruz caught up to her before she could push outside to safety and fresh air. "What is going on?"

"I don't feel so well. Can you bring the food back to the room?" She braced herself for his endless questions of what was wrong and ways she could fix her problems.

"Sure."

She almost asked him to repeat himself because she wasn't expecting him to agree so freely. "Which room?"

He handed her the key with the room number on it and turned away. She could either follow through with this abrupt departure or return to the booth and stick it out. She pushed through the door.

The night air clung to her skin and wouldn't let go now that she had stepped into it. She could barely breathe out here either, but this time it was the humidity and not her anxiety. More storms were imminent. She checked her phone for the latest weather update. Nothing was predicted until the early hours of the morning. They would be able to get a few hours of sleep before hitting the road.

If she slept at all.

CHAPTER 7

CRUZ KNOCKED on the motel room door. He hadn't thought to get another key and by the time he returned to the office, the door was locked tight. Rue, the office manager, had gone home to her husband Ralph and their five cats.

Ever since Ayla slid out of the diner's booth with running in her eyes, he couldn't get a handle on what was going on between them. Delivering that baby had been one crazy ride. He had never seen a birth before even while working as an EMT in college. He had hoped his baby would have been his first. Who knew if he would ever have children now? What was once a tangible goal was so far out of reach, he might as well ask rain not to come out of a cumulonimbus cloud.

The entire time young Erin had pushed and grunted, he had hoped sharing the birth with Ayla would bring them closer. It had done the exact opposite. From the moment they returned to the car, mother and baby safely on the ambulance and others rescued with their help, she had folded in on herself until she made a run for it from the diner. Taking off was Ayla's go-to response. He should be used to it by now, but he wasn't, and it hurt. Delivering that baby with her only reminded him of exactly how much he still loved her.

The door swung open and brushed his thoughts away. Ayla stepped aside to let him pass. She had changed out of her wide-leg pants and tank top to a loose t-shirt and shorts. Her hair was piled up on her head and fatigue weighed down her lids.

The motel room smelled stale and old as if it had been locked up tight for years. Sad curtains hung limp from a black rod above the window and the sagging bed was dressed in bland beige, matching the walls, the carpet, and the crooked nondescript artwork on the wall.

"Hey. Here's the food." He held up the white plastic bag and admonished himself for stating the obvious.

She took the cardboard drink carrier from him and placed it on the table. He put the bag beside the drinks. Echoes of the interstate punctuated the silence in the room.

"Thanks for bringing it here. It was so hot in the diner. It was giving me a headache." She pulled out the burgers, placing them on the table beside the drinks, then bit into a fry with a gleeful groan. She wiped her mouth with a napkin and balled it in her fist.

She always did that when she ate. No matter how many napkins she used, they all ended up in a crumpled ball as if she was angry at each one. What was she so angry about? Was she still angry at him for leaving her because he hadn't the ability to care for her when he was trying to save himself? Or was she angry at the weather because it wouldn't cooperate? None of the answers mattered. They didn't change anything. He loved her just the same.

He could use a beer or a bourbon. If he wasn't so tired, he might go drive around and find an all-night liquor store. Something about the disarray of Radiant told him the town would most likely have one of those. Hell, maybe two.

"You're not fooling me. You didn't have a headache. You ran out to get that blanket earlier because you didn't want to be in the room with Erin and her baby, and you ran out of the diner because you didn't want to be with me. Just say it. You're sorry you asked me to come along."

That thought had grabbed hold of him and gnawed at his insides all day. She had said she wanted him to help her, but she didn't. He was her last resort. He should have figured that out when he realized the water in the basement was only a ploy to get him to drive two hours and give up his hiking trip. Mason and Ryder were wrong about Ayla wanting to come back. He had foolishly hoped they were onto something.

"You're right about the first part, but wrong about the second." She flopped down in the straight-backed chair, then took a big bite out of the burger. Her gaze remained on the food the whole time.

He sat opposite her, but he wasn't hungry any longer. "What are you saying?"

Her gaze snapped up. "What is confusing about that? I didn't want to watch a baby being born."

"But it's a miracle."

"Yes, it is. A miracle that should have been mine. Do you know every time I see a pregnant woman I walk in the opposite direction or cross the street? I can't be near them."

"We've been through an ordeal." After losing the baby, he kept moving forward. He didn't want to dwell on what had happened. If he did that, he might have lost his mind. But he hadn't been the one carrying the baby. Reminders weren't the same for him.

"Don't patronize me." She jumped out of the chair and scurried around the bed to the other side of the room.

He pushed out of the chair too but didn't go to her. The room was too small for all their problems.

Having space from each other hadn't helped them either. Maybe they were beyond repair, and he needed to admit it.

"I'm not condescending to you. No one blames you for how you feel."

"You did. You blamed me for storm chasing while I was pregnant, and you blamed me for going back out after. I didn't know what to do with myself after. I didn't fit in my own skin because my baby was gone, and I caused it to happen. I needed you to understand why I had to go, but you left me." Fire and tears burned in her tired eyes.

He opened his mouth to defend himself, but he shut it. He had blamed her. He had never said the words, but Ayla knew him as well as he knew her. Blame oozed from his pores. He had been angry at the world, angrier than he had ever been at the atrocities he saw in battle because this tragedy had befallen him. Selfish as that may have been, he wanted to dump the blame anywhere and Ayla had provided a good target.

"I never blamed you. You didn't mean to get caught in that down draft and tossed for yards. The pain from the loss... I couldn't breathe... I was terrified I'd lose you next. It hasn't been easy for me either." He sat on the edge of the bed, held his head in his hands, and stared at his boots.

After he had walked out, they had barely spoken. He hadn't wanted to go near any of the hurt by having long conversations that dragged up the past. He had held tight to his convictions, certain he was right, but after watching that baby today, something broke open in him.

"Why didn't you say that sooner?" She wiped her face with the back of her hand.

"I couldn't." He had no excuses.

"You never let me forget, if I hadn't been in the car, we would have a family."

"I never said that." But he had thought it, and he hated himself for having those thoughts. He loved his wife, but he couldn't stop himself from following that evil thread down a dead-end road until he was sick inside.

"You didn't have to." She threw her hands in the air. "I thought it too. When you walked out the door and walked out of my life, I knew it was my fault. You wouldn't have left me if you believed otherwise. You would have been waiting for me."

"How much did you want me to take? My heart was already broken, and then you left, risking your life on the heels of what had happened. I thought you were trying to punish me for being upset, for wanting our baby."

"No, Cruz, I wasn't trying to punish you. I was trying to save myself. I wanted our baby too."

"Why did you jump out of the car earlier today when we came up on the tornado? Does it have to do with what you've been through?" The pieces started to fit together for him. Before the accident, when she saw a storm, her eyes lit up with a manic energy. She was addicted to the adrenaline rush of chasing. He had seen it in others, even in men doing battle. He never liked it when a man on his team enjoyed the fighting too much. That man could end up being dangerous.

"Don't make me talk about it."

"Could it be that you were also trying to hurt yourself?"

She shook her head, but her face crumpled. Her lips twisted into an ugly grimace and red blotches broke out on her skin as if a poisonous rash had grabbed her.

He went to her and pulled her into his arms. She burst into racking sobs and held on to him. They stood that way while she cried long and hard as if an overflowing, raging river of despair burst through a barrier. He didn't want to think about all the time they had wasted apart. If they had only had this conversation sooner, but neither of them was in any shape to do it before. Time had given them enough space that they could do it now. Time and a little baby named Cruz Alexander who was delivered on the heels of a mean and angry tornado.

～

AYLA FISTED the back of Cruz's shirt in her hands. As if someone had flipped a newly found switch, she cried enough tears to produce a tropical cyclone. Snot ran down her plugged nose. Her face would be covered in ugly red blotches, her eyes swollen. Cruz's shirt was wet with her bawling and mucus. She disgusted herself. How could he not pull away and run from her? She needed a tissue and broke away from Cruz to blow her nose in the bathroom. She splashed water on her face, then cupped her hand to slurp some for her dry throat. A glance in the mirror sent her back into the bedroom. No need to investigate her haphazard appearance. She had never been a pretty crier.

She returned to the bedroom. He pulled her back into his arms. She went without argument.

"It's anxiety."

"What is?" He held her close.

"I'm having panic attacks when I get near a storm, any kind of storm, not just tornados."

His hands stilled on her back. "For how long?"

"Since the first time I went out after the baby. That's why I don't have the footage and why Austin quit on me." She kept her cheek against his chest and avoided having to look at him. Telling the truth was easier with her eyes closed.

"This whole time? Why didn't you say anything sooner?" He remained still as if he too couldn't make eye contact.

"I wasn't ready to tell you. But after the baby today, and the way I acted, you deserved to know." She held her breath and counted to ten, waiting for him to explode.

"You thought I'd be mad." It wasn't a question.

"I thought you wouldn't come with me today if I told you the whole story." She had to see him and eased out of the embrace. He looked at her with a sadness in his eyes.

"We're a mess, you and me." He sat on the edge of the bed.

"I think so." She sat beside him.

"I might not have come because I don't want you to keep putting yourself in harm's way. But I wouldn't have ever wanted you to go out alone. Never again. Promise me that."

"Never again. I'm sorry I didn't tell you." She put her hand on his solid thigh. Whenever she was near him, she needed to touch him. She used to walk up to him anywhere in the house and put her hands on him just because she could.

"I haven't exactly been a good partner," he said.

"So, you're not mad?"

"No, I am not mad. Are you taking anything for the anxiety?" He took her hand and laced their fingers together.

"I hated the way the pills made me feel." She had tried for a month or two but stopped. She was always fine unless a storm had come up and she was out in it.

"I'm sorry you're going through this," he said against her hair. His hands rubbed her back, and she sank into him. Her muscles unlocked some of their tension. In his arms was the only place she wanted to be.

She had needed this release when she woke up in the hospital all those months ago, but the tears hadn't come, and Cruz walked around a shell of himself, lost to the here and now. His eyes had grown vacant. He would stare off into space, as if his mind had found a better place to exist. She hadn't known how to reach for him, and he hadn't the energy to grab on to her and tug her back.

"I'm sorry you are too," she said.

He placed a kiss on her cheek. She cupped his face and kept him close. If she turned her face just a little, their lips would touch.

"Are you hungry? The food is getting cold." He slipped away and set the table with their food.

His muscles flexed under his shirt as he arranged the containers. He needed something to organize, orchestrate, command. That was the man she loved, always giving commands and everyone listening to him. He was a good leader because of his ability to sway people his way with kindness.

He always kept busy when life became too hard for him. He would return from duty and disappear for hours to either play hockey with Mason and Ryder, to ski in the winter, or to hike any time of year. He had never asked her to go along on those trips. She had let him have his space. Maybe giving him space had been a mistake. Now, they didn't know how to talk to each other.

"Those pants look good on you." She hadn't meant to say that, but the words found their way into the silence. His pants cupped his butt, and she couldn't pull her gaze away or keep her mouth shut. Plus that lingering kiss... it had to mean something.

He turned and gave her a small smile. She had never been cautious where he was concerned except after her accident. From the first moment they had met, she poured out her feelings to him about everything from school to her politics to how hot he was. He had fit with her, and she had taken him for granted, expecting him to always be there no matter what hell she was going through or putting him through.

Outside, the wind played its soundtrack of howls and whines, shoving itself against the small motel as a reminder of who, in the end, would be the strongest. Storms weren't far away, threatening to rip them from this room and send them on another chase. If she had any other options, she would leave the storms alone. Cruz was all she wanted. Something so simple was so damn hard and complicated.

Staring at him with his smooth skin and dark eyes, a magnetic energy—that Cruz most likely did not feel—tugged at her core. She tried to resist its strength, planting her bare feet firmly on the thin carpet, but she was a sinking ship in a Category 5 hurricane. Her body took control over the logic in her brain, and she cleared the space between them, jumping into his arms.

He caught her in time, keeping her from landing on her butt, and started to say something, but she stopped him by sticking her tongue in his mouth.

CHAPTER 8

AYLA RAN her fingers through Cruz's soft hair. She wanted her hands all over him, as they still stood by the table in the motel room with her legs around him and their mouths joined.

He kissed her back, his tongue swooping her mouth and sending shivers over her skin. No one kissed like this man. She didn't have a lot to compare him to since they'd met in college, but while they were apart, she tried to go on a couple of dates, always judging the men against her husband. They were never as smart or funny. And certainly not as sexy.

Cruz eased back and planted her on her feet. "Uh... what was that?"

She backed away as if she'd been pushed. Heat climbed into her face and not from the make-out session. "I was kissing you. Have you already forgotten what kissing is?"

"Funny. Why are you kissing me?" He regarded her with a coolness in his eyes.

"I took a risk. One of my risks. Not one of yours." She could remind him about how long he debated to ask her out on their first date and then how long it took him to kiss her. He had calculated all of her possible reactions, but that would do no good. He didn't want to be with her in that way any longer. Too many months had gone by without any type of intimacy between them. Too many unsaid words.

"I don't want to start something that we will regret later," he said.

"But you want to start something?" She took a step closer, hoping for an affirmative to her question. She didn't want to think about regrets. She had plenty of those always getting in her way.

"You were upset. You might be mistaking those feelings with your feelings for me."

"No." She should back away from this, but she could no more deny how much she wanted him than she could deny her curly hair, her love of photography, or the increased winds outside their room that scared her less because Cruz was here.

"No, you aren't upset, or no you're not mixing up your feelings?" His eyes narrowed.

"Yes, I was upset. There's no pretending I didn't

111

slobber all over your shirt. Sorry about that, by the way. And no, I'm not confused about what I want. I want you, Cruz. Only you."

He held her gaze and his tongue.

"Please say something." Or it would be a very long night and she really didn't want to sleep in the car. He wouldn't make her do that. She would be the one who wouldn't be able to be in the same room with him all night if he completely rejected her.

"You want to have sex with me?"

"For a smart, accomplished guy, you can be a little thickheaded. Would this help?" She pulled her shirt over her head and dropped it on the floor. She stood before him in her bra and shorts.

He sucked in a breath. "Sex changes everything."

"I believe you said that to me right before we did it the first time." She closed the space between them and looked up to meet his gaze.

"I don't remember that." He ran a finger over her shoulder with the tattoo. His light touch tickled her skin, but he dropped his hand just as quickly.

She wanted him to continue to touch her in all the places that missed him most. "Trust me. We were in your dorm room. Your roommate had gone home for the weekend. I'd been wanting you to touch me for weeks, but you hadn't even kissed me." She hadn't been completely sure he liked her as a girlfriend. She had to know before she had lost her mind. She might've been rushing things a little back then, but she was unable to wait—like now.

"I didn't want you to feel pressured."

"You wanted to make certain I liked you that way."

"That too." His smile burst across his face.

She went to him and wrapped her arms around his neck and snuggled against him. He placed his hands on the small of her back.

"What do you say, Cruz? Is this what you want?" She swayed her hips against him.

"Is this a *one for the road* kind of thing?"

She hadn't considered a one-night stand. It might be all either of them could give in the end, but she didn't want to muse over any of that now. Her body hummed for him. In the light of day, they could figure out the rest.

"Do we have to make plans for the future, tonight? Can we live in the moment?"

"I don't know what to do here. We've been going down the road of splitting up for a while now."

"Let's not think about it. We don't need to have all the answers right now. Tonight I just want to make love with you."

"I can't." He pulled open the door and left her alone.

∾

CRUZ PACED the parking lot away from the window of their motel room. Wind kicked up and rolled some trash across the asphalt. Only a few cars dotted the spots by the diner. Their vehicle was the only one by a motel room. Looked as if they were the only ones here.

He pulled out his phone to call one of his friends but shoved it back into his pocket. What was he going to say to Mason or Ryder? *Ayla wants to screw, and I just turned her down.* He could hear the laughing now.

He wanted to make love with her. It was never screwing. Not for him. He should insist they discuss their future and what tonight would mean if they still went their separate ways, but he was tired of the conversations that circled back to the same spot. Maybe two people who had been through an ordeal couldn't get away from it. The tragedy would always hang over their heads like— *dare he say it*—storm clouds.

Her earthy smell still clung to him. Mixed with the scent of rain in the air, all he wanted to do was march back inside that room and make love to her all night. But if she walked out on him again, he wouldn't be able to push the hurt away a second time.

Could he do what she asked and live in this moment? Could he put the future on hold and for once in his very planned life take a risk?

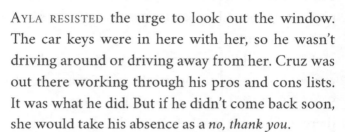

AYLA RESISTED the urge to look out the window. The car keys were in here with her, so he wasn't driving around or driving away from her. Cruz was out there working through his pros and cons lists. It was what he did. But if he didn't come back soon, she would take his absence as a *no, thank you*.

They should iron out their differences and really talk about what they both wanted, but she was too tired to talk right now. Today's events weighed on her and shook her to her core. Watching a baby being born was pure joy, but also total torture. She needed space from the hurt and regret. In the light of day, she would try again to tell him how sorry she was and that she wanted another chance. Right after they caught up to the next storm and she took her photos. On the way back to Aurora, that's when she would risk the conversation she had been avoiding for months.

Time ticked forward, mocking her from the screen on her phone, and still no Cruz. He might've gone to the diner, or he might've hitched. No, not hitched. He would never do that, but he might call Ryder and ask him to come and get him. That would take hours. Could he be that repulsed by the idea that she wanted to sleep with him again? She liked to think not.

She brushed her teeth and climbed into bed.

Her legs slipped under the cool sheets. If he did come back in while she was awake, she would pretend to be asleep and save them both some embarrassment.

Sleep would never come as long as he didn't return. Too many thoughts churned in her mind. Some of which had to do with her career or lack thereof. She still needed those photos and videos and she needed Cruz to help her. Okay, jumping into his arms had been a hasty mistake. She should have thought about the long-term ramifications of offering sex. She would apologize for that too and keep her hands to herself.

The door creaked open and spilled a muted glow into the room from the parking lot lights. She turned her back to him.

"Ayla, are you awake?" The click of the lock and the rattling of the safety chain echoed in the air.

She focused on the wind and not his footsteps by the bed or the shift of the mattress under his weight.

"Ayla?" His voice was a whisper and if they were outside, that fierce wind would have grabbed it and taken it away, just like it took so many things without asking.

Tears threatened again. She was a mess, lying here in the dark, aching for the life she had with the man she loved and wondering if her work would ever mean anything after all she lost to accomplish it.

"I'm awake." She could never lie to him. She didn't understand women who did just that. She had wanted to tell Cruz everything from the moment she met him. That hadn't changed. But she kept her back to him, just the same.

He slid onto the bed and curled against her. His arm wrapped around her waist and pulled her to him. She didn't resist, but snuggled in the way they had a thousand times before. She was safe in his arms with his large, strong body almost covering hers.

"We don't have to talk. We never have to say a word. In the morning, I will take you to find your storm. After that, you can decide what you want, and I will do whatever that is. Go or stay. It's up to you. I've made enough decisions to last a thousand years, always trying to save as many lives as possible. I was often right and still people were hurt. I don't want to hurt you, and I don't want to be hurt again. When I'm with you, that's all there is—just you. So, for tonight, and for tonight only, I won't ask any questions. I won't make any demands or decisions. Whatever you want is what I'll do."

She turned in his arms so she could face him. Holding him like this started an ache low in her belly.

The room was dark, turning his handsome

features she knew by heart into a silhouette. "Turn on the lamp," she said.

"You want the light on?"

"I want to see your face."

He reached behind him and clicked on the light. She blinked against the glare, but he came into focus. He was really there. He had returned to her. Cruz wrapped his arm around her again but didn't pull her any closer.

"Is this better?" he said.

"Much. Just one more night." She would worry about tomorrow then. For now, he was here.

He kissed her then and all thoughts of broken promises made in the dark were obliterated. His tongue commanded her attention, and his hands found their way under her shirt. He rubbed her nipple between his fingers. A moan slipped from her lips. He wasn't close enough. She needed him closer and wrapped her leg around his waist, trying to pull him in, to keep him from getting too far away.

She didn't want to waste time with lots of foreplay and teasing. They had played that game before, and though she loved the way he could coax her to the edge without sending her over until she begged him, her insides hummed to feel him inside her.

His mouth found her neck and nipped his way to her collarbone. She fumbled with the button of his pants until it broke free under her touch and she could push the fabric to his ankles.

He sat up and tore his shirt over his head. Then he tossed his pants to the floor. She yanked off her top and let him soak her in.

"Nothing compares to you naked," he said. "Not the most beautiful sunset or lightning storm."

She climbed to her knees to be the same height as him, then pressed her chest to his. He cupped her bottom and pulled her against his erection, straining under his boxer-briefs. She held his gaze for a brief moment, but the need to be connected took control.

His hands slid over her bottom and back up to her shoulders. Her mind spun with memories of them making love as if a movie played in her head. Desire whirled like tornado clouds. A tornado was inside her now, growing until it could explode.

"Will you turn around?" he said between kisses on her neck. His hands already began shifting her away from him.

She did as he asked, and he tugged her underwear down her legs until they were at her knees, holding her legs in place.

"That won't do." He tugged them the rest of the way and tossed them to the floor with the other garments. He did the same with his own.

He ran his tongue down her spine. Pressure built inside her and she was powerless to its strength. She placed her hands on the wall above the headboard to keep from falling over. His mouth returned to her neck, but now his full erection pressed against her. His hand ran down her front. First over her breast, then her abdomen until it dipped low into her heat.

"God, Ayla, you're incredible." His other hand caressed her breast.

The storm inside her pulsed and raged, matching the wind outside. Somewhere in the distance, thunder rolled across the sky and through her. Cruz's hand slid in and out, lifting her into the vortex higher and higher until she could look down at them on the bed.

"Harder," she said through labored breaths.

Instead of answering her plea, he slowed down. "Not yet. It's too soon," he said.

He tortured her in the most amazing way, but it had been too many months since she had been with a man. She wanted to hurry as if her body chased its own storm that might slip away if she took too long.

"I'm ready," she said.

"I want to make sure." He removed his hand completely, and she groaned in frustration.

"Let me touch you." She tried to turn around, to turn the tables. If she could make him as aroused as she was, he would not want to wait either.

"Not yet." He gripped her waist and kept her away from him.

"I thought you were done making decisions." She tossed a smile over her shoulder.

"I like the kind of decisions that make you hot." He kissed her neck again.

His hands returned to her hips, but only held her in place against him. For good measure, she rubbed her backside against him, and he moaned.

With a little sweet revenge on her side, she slipped her hand up his thigh, but the angle was wrong, and she couldn't get what she wanted.

He returned her hand to the wall. "Stay that way. I like you pinned."

The ache went into her bones. "Touch me."

His hand returned to her sweet spot. His finger entered and slid away in a slow, smooth motion until his touch became too much and not enough at the same time.

"Are you ready for me?" He continued to stroke her.

"Yes." Her breath came in short bursts. The swirling inside her moved faster. She would not last much longer.

"I don't think you are." His other hand massaged her breast while his lips played tricks against her neck. "Or am I wrong?"

"Very wrong." She didn't want to waste energy with words. Staying up on her knees grew more difficult with his increased touch. Her arms shook as she held herself in place while he directed her desire upward.

"Shit." His hands dropped and his body moved from hers, taking all the heat with him.

She twisted to face him. Her heart dropped into her stomach. "What? What's wrong?"

"Are you still on the pill?"

"You stopped to ask me that?" What was he thinking?

"I don't want any... you know... issues later."

She stared at him and tried to focus on this conversation with both of them naked in the lamp-light. Once again, he was the one thinking ahead. "No. I never went back on. There hasn't been any reason."

"You haven't had sex since us?" He arched a brow.

"Don't let it go to your head." She sat on her heels. The rest of her heat slipped away like a funnel cloud climbing back into the sky.

"I have a condom. I'll grab it." He hopped off the bed and found his wallet.

She bit back the question of what he was doing with one. He was an attractive man that any woman would be lucky to take to bed. He had a healthy desire for sex, but the idea of another woman with him tore her in two.

"How many women?" Words always betrayed

her. Any answer would haunt her because he was with another woman. She wanted to be the only one.

"You don't want to talk about this now."

"Tell me or I'm putting my clothes back on and going to bed. And don't lie."

He let out a long breath and ran a hand over his face. "Okay. One. I hated every second of it because she wasn't you."

"Then why did you do it?" She forced the image of Cruz above another woman out of her head. She would never be able to get back to where they were if she hung on to the idea too long.

"Mason thought it was the only way I'd get over you." He closed the space between them and kissed her neck.

"Of course, Mason. And you listened to him." She put her hands on his shoulders and pushed him away.

"I was desperate. I tried drinking you away. That didn't work. I tried working myself to death, but you were still everywhere. I thought maybe a woman…"

"Never mind. I don't need to know. Your life is your business. We're separated. I get it." But her heart didn't understand at all.

"She didn't mean anything to me. I even called her by your name." He sat on the edge of the bed.

"You did not." She tried not to laugh, but the image made her want to giggle.

"I did. I'm sorry. I wouldn't have said anything, but you asked."

"And you don't lie." She sat beside him.

"That's our deal." He held her hand.

It was. They had made that promise from the start. No matter how hard the truth was, they told it.

She kissed him again because she wanted to get back to where they were before he pulled away, and kissing him could erase the thoughts of him with someone else. As long as he was here with her, no other woman existed.

He eased out of the kiss and put on the condom.

"Take it off." This was all wrong. The images of another woman were still there as if she had walked right into the room with them. And she had because Ayla had invited her with her stupid questions.

"What?"

"I don't want to do it with you covered." She hated the idea, in fact.

"Ayla, we don't want to take a chance. People make babies at our age."

"I can't do it, knowing you were with another woman wearing that thing." They had never done it using a condom. Well, maybe a couple of times, but it wasn't their thing. She went on the pill before they had sex the first time. Cruz was her first, and she was his second. They were young and not worried about diseases.

"Not this exact one." He choked out a laugh.

She tried not to laugh too and encourage him. "Please. Just you and me and nothing between us." She leaned in and gripped him.

He sucked in a breath and held her gaze. She slid the condom off. Her fingers traveled the length of him until her hand was wrapped around his full width. He pulsed against her touch, sending her back up into the clouds.

They kissed again. No more words were needed. She would deal with the aftermath of this unprotected storm at a later date, if at all. This was a risk worth taking. The choices of her actions would land where they would, and she would clean up her mess, if necessary. For now, she wanted Cruz inside her the way he was meant to be.

She leaned back on the pillows, and he followed her, brushing her hair away from her face with a tender touch. He entered her then, and they rocked together until they reached a height high enough to steal her breath. Their bodies fit as if they were made for each other. No other man would be right for her in the same way. How could she fall hard for more than one person? Impossible. If all she would get was one night, she had better make it worth it.

She pushed her hips up to meet his, wrapping her legs around his waist to give him more room. Each thrust brought her to the edge of a familiar cliff, one she had fallen off a thousand times before.

He held her gaze. "Tell me when."

He was waiting for her. He always waited. Tears filled her eyes. Only he hadn't waited when she needed him most. He had walked out the door, leaving her alone.

"Now." She pushed up higher and arched her back.

They plummeted together, his face buried in her neck, landing on the debris of their mistakes.

CHAPTER 9

AYLA SLEPT in Cruz's arms. He held her close as her chest moved with each breath. Her soft curves smoothed out his hard edges. She always fit against him as if she were made for him, but life had stabbed them in the eye when they weren't looking and made them forget they were a team once.

Thunder's roar shook the motel. Another storm snuck up while they lay here, holding each other. It wasn't on them yet, but it would be and they would have to chase it while it was angry and dangerous.

He should check the radar for the possibility of a supercell that could turn into a tornado, but he didn't want to disturb Ayla or himself, if he were being honest.

Their lovemaking had resembled what it was before she became pregnant and they still had a bit of a carefreeness about their time in the bedroom.

She had rocked his world from the first time to the last. He had no idea sex could stay good for so long, but it had. He only regretted allowing her to take off the condom. He wasn't ready to be a father, after everything they had been through together. He hadn't realized that until this moment. They might not make it after all this was over, and then they could be tied together because of a baby. No child should grow up with parents who don't trust each other.

He wiped a hand over his face and slipped out of bed, careful not to wake her. He grabbed his pants and a shirt and went outside. The air was thick and wet. The humidity had increased in the last couple of hours like a pot of boiling water. White lightning cracked open the dark sky. For a brief moment, the road was lit then gone as if it had never been there. Thunder followed six seconds later. The storm was close. He turned and looked back at the motel room. A storm had already arrived.

If he were a smoker, he imagined this would be one of those times someone would light up. He sure as hell could use a beer. The diner was dark. Everyone in Radiant had gone home for the night. He might be the only one awake.

He didn't regret making love with her. He had wanted her since he showed up at her house earlier. She wanted him too. He needed a plan on what would happen after they caught the storm. And what if, on some small chance, they made a baby tonight? Did he really want Ayla up against another tornado if she was carrying his baby for a second time? What if they didn't get out of the way in time?

What a mess he made because he had allowed logic and reason to be run over by lust. What the hell was wrong with him?

He went inside and checked the weather app. There was still time before they had to get back in the car. She might want to go now, if she saw the maps. He would let her sleep for a little longer. He wasn't sure if it was for her good—or his.

AYLA LEAPED out of the bed, trying to get her bearings. Right, she was in a motel and she and Cruz had made crazy love.

Rain pelted the roof of the motel, and wind screamed against the windows. Cruz snored, lying on his back in the bed. He was dressed again. When had that happened?

She hurried into her clothes, then grabbed her phone. A line of storms was forming in the east. They needed to get there in time for her to film.

"Cruz, get up." She shook him.

He grunted but didn't wake.

"Lieutenant Colonel Lacerda, report for duty." She gave him a good shove this time and he sat straight up.

"What the hell?" He rubbed his eyes with the heels of his hands. "What time is it?"

"It's a little after six. We need to hurry. There's a line of supercells forming. I don't want to miss this one." She tossed some things into her bag.

"Do I have time for a shower?" He swung his legs over the side of the bed.

"No. We need to hit the road now. We can stop for coffee along the way."

He went into the bathroom and splashed water on his face. She bit back the words to tell him to hurry his ass up, but waited for him by the door instead.

He kissed her on the cheek. "Good morning, by the way."

"Good morning. Are you ready?" She stepped outside, not waiting for an answer. Last night was last night, and it had been wonderful, but this morning she was a storm chaser on a mission.

"Where to?" Cruz slid into the driver's side of the car.

She hopped in beside him. "East. Take the interstate east."

"Buckle up." He pulled out of the parking lot and onto the road leading to the interstate.

She gave a final look at the motel she would

never be able to forget. Hopefully, it didn't become the motel that haunted her.

The landscape flew past as Cruz put miles between them and the motel. Ayla fought the uncomfortable buzzing under her skin, but the anxiety was winning as they approached the storm.

He pulled off the interstate at the next exit and followed the roads. "I need the GPS," he said. "I don't know the way these streets go, and I don't want us to follow one to a dead end. We need to know there's an escape route."

She pulled up the map on her phone and placed it on the holder, facing Cruz. Not every road was marked on GPS. Some roads had never been paved and led nowhere. Those were the roads that didn't show up, but a chaser could find themselves on one and find trouble.

"It's not far now," she said.

"Are you okay?"

"I'm good. I can do this." She had to do this. She was out of options. He wouldn't stick around long enough to find more storms if this cluster didn't work out. He had given her forty-eight hours and she doubted he would extend that because he had a decent orgasm.

"You don't have to." He stole a glance at her.

"I do. Please don't try and talk me out of it. I need your support and your ability to drive fast."

"If you don't think you can handle going up to

that tornado, at any point, you say so and I'll get you out of there. You don't have to be a hero."

"Said from a hero himself."

"I'm not a hero, Ayla. I was doing my job." He made a right-hand turn.

"And I'm doing mine."

"But your job is dangerous."

"Here we go again. Can you stop talking and just drive?" She did not want to have this conversation again, not when her insides started that hornet's nest buzzing thing it did.

"Fine. No more talking." Anger pinched his features, but she didn't respond. She had to focus on staying calm.

The wall cloud appeared before them as if for their benefit, filling the sky with its dense gray mass and ready to drop its hell on the ground. The nebula moved with deliberation as if it had all the time in the world to wreak havoc on the land below. Clouds rotated, kicking up a strong wind that blew dirt and grass into the air on a swirl that resembled brown flames. Wind screeched and shoved the car, but the vehicle remained on the road. Rain poured down on them. The windshield wipers worked overtime.

"Get close." She had to yell to be heard above the wind now. She fought the bile coming up from her empty stomach. She wasn't sure if she could get out of the car and point her camera. Images of her accident invaded her thoughts, distracting her from the job.

She had driven alone that night. Her partner had bailed at the last second. The roads had confused her as she made turn after turn. She had been trying to get around the tornado to where a better shot might be, but everywhere she went, the massive funnel waited for her, blocking the way.

A wave of nausea had washed over her. The tornado had trapped her. She had called out for Cruz, but the only thing that came back was the sinister laugh of the wind.

Now, she stole a glance at Cruz. He sat hunched over the wheel, his gaze focused out the window. Visibility was getting worse. She had to try to fight the panic and be brave. She made a silent plea with any higher power that would listen. If she got the footage she needed and could save her reputation, she would promise not to do this again.

Cruz took another turn and put them on a dirt road with the tornado to their left. He could reverse out if the tornado came too close. The dirt road would work against them, though. They could get stuck in mud or in a spot where a puddle was deep. They just had to stay out of the tornado's path. They would never be able to outrun it.

He pulled over to the side of the road and threw the car in park. "This is close enough."

"I need you to get closer."

"No, damn it. You're close enough. Just point your camera up and take the photos."

The white cloud funnel dropped from the sky in a neat cylinder and hit the ground, tearing up the dirt and crops. It was an official tornado now, chewing through the fields of corn and wheat and tearing the plants from the ground as if they were nothing more than short-rooted weeds. If the town was around here, there would be more destruction like Sugar had been.

She didn't have time to waste and grabbed her camera. From her position, the angle of the tornado was all wrong for filming. Nothing unusual or magical happened in the viewfinder. Storm chasers all over the place had footage like this one. She needed something more spectacular. Maybe on the other side the sky would have spots of blue or streams of sun intertwined with the cloud.

"Can you go around it?"

"I won't risk it from here. The tornado will intersect with the road ahead. I'm not going to try and race it. Taking another route might drive us farther away before you can get close and you'll miss the whole thing. It's now or never."

He didn't understand the life of a chaser. He got it logically because he was brilliant and a scientist, but emotionally, chasing was beyond him. She couldn't explain how it felt to him now.

"You can get around it. It's done all the time. But not by you because you think what I do is crazy."

Other photographers would race to the tornado and run around it, hoping to find what they were looking for. Storm chasers wouldn't take no for an answer from the weather because they wanted to either throw their scientific instruments into the tornado or document it with photos and videos. Cruz only wanted to watch from afar, where it was safe.

"It is crazy. Every one of you in this field is nuts. Ever since that ridiculous reality television show aired, amateur storm chasers have popped up everywhere. People are getting hurt. Not today. Not you. Get out and take some photos."

"I'm not an amateur, damn it."

"You're a photographer. Not a scientist trying to collect data from what goes on inside a tornado. Even that isn't enough of a reason to risk your life. It's now or never. If you don't get out and take some photos, I'm going to turn this car around."

She wanted to argue further, but time worked against her. She hopped out of the car and aimed, clicking and pointing. She would search through her collected treasures later like a child with seashells in a bucket. The winners would be found away from the storm.

Rain soaked through her clothes, sticking them to her. Golf ball-sized hail dropped from the sky, causing her to duck. She shivered as cold raindrops slid down her back. Her vision blurred from the dirt kicking up, or maybe it was her nerves. She had to plant her feet wide to keep from falling over, and still the wind pummeled her, undeterred by her determination to have the last word. She was closer to the vortex than she realized. Cruz had done what she asked. She should be thrilled.

Cruz turned the car around so they would face the right way when they took off again and save valuable seconds they would need. He called to her from the car, but she couldn't hear him over the wind. Lightning flashed, startling her. Her brain yelled run.

Her wet hair slapped her in the face. Her hands were cold and shook as the tornado moved across the road in front of her.

A scream reached up from her throat, but she swallowed it back down. Her vision blurred again. She couldn't tell what she took photos of exactly, but she had to keep trying. Fear and stubbornness warred within her. She couldn't lose to terror or to nature.

"Ayla, get back in the car."

She ignored Cruz and switched the camera to video mode. She needed more video for the documentary, but her hands continued to shake. Her unsteady grip fumbled with the equipment. She should have grabbed her tripod. Her mind continued to work against her.

"Ayla, it's changed directions. Come on. We have to get out of here now."

Its rotation hypnotized her, the untouchable beauty of something deadly. She couldn't leave now. Her camera had to capture the wind turning on a hinge of disaster. A few more seconds and she would have the perfect video piece, wind and rain carving their way through the ground, dropkicking anything—wanted or not—in their path. The tornado was the master out here and her simply its servant. She pointed the camera skyward for a wide shot of the thick opaque wall cloud at the top of the funnel. This was it. This was the moment she waited for.

"Ayla, damn it. Now. We're out of time." Cruz's voice carried into the wind as if he were a red-tailed hawk, screeching at her and her carelessness.

The tornado turned toward her as if aware of being watched. She stared up at it, frozen in her spot. Mad wind and more hail almost knocked her off her feet. She swayed and dropped the camera from her numb fingers. Cruz locked his arms around her in a viselike grip from behind and carried her to the car.

"No, stop. My camera." She kicked her legs to fight his hold, but he was too strong.

"Get in the car. Forget the camera." He dropped her into the passenger seat.

"I need my camera." She tried to climb out, but he shut the door and ran around the front, throwing himself inside before her wet and cold hands could work the door handle. He pulled her shirt and dumped her back in the seat.

"Go back." She hit him in the shoulder.

The tornado came up behind them like a predator. Cruz floored it, putting only yards between them. The engine struggled to drag the car forward against the wind and through the ruts in the dirt road. The wipers were no match for the rain, turning the view out the front into a wicked blur. She glanced out the back window. The funnel took her camera and sucked it into its core. All her work was gone.

"I hate you." She swatted at her hair sticking to her face. She was soaked through and shivering.

"Hate me all you want. Another five seconds and it would have been you in that tornado." A vein popped out on the side of his neck. A raindrop ran over it.

"I lost my work." She pressed against the door, wanting to be as far from him as possible.

"I'll get you another camera." His knuckles turned white as he gripped the wheel.

"I don't need you to buy me a camera. I need you to let me take my pictures. You don't understand. You are the best in your field. But me, I'm always screwing up. I have to prove myself." And she had failed, again. This time she was so close she could taste the win, but now it was ripped from her hands.

"You don't have to prove yourself to anyone but yourself." He stole a glance, but quickly looked back on the road made difficult to see by the torrential rain.

"That's easy for you to say. Your father is proud of you." A puddle formed on the floor by her feet.

He stole another glance in her direction. "Is that what this is all about? You want your father to be proud of you?"

"No. I don't know." She threw her hands in the air in frustration. She did know. She didn't want to say it out loud.

"He's gone, Ayla. He can't come back from the grave to pat you on the shoulder for risking your life in severe weather."

"I know that." At least on a logical level, she did.

Her entire life her father had compared her to her older brothers. Vincent and Markus could do no wrong where their dad was concerned. But her... her grades were never good enough; if she made the team, why wasn't she the captain? If she came in second, why wasn't she first? Her room was always a mess, her hair unruly, her mouth sassy. She would watch her father call one of her brothers in to watch a football game, then later as they became men to share a scotch. Her father talked military tactics, world history, and government with her brothers. When she tried to talk to him about any of that, he told her he was busy with work, go help her mother. Nothing she did ever pleased him.

"Do you know what I have told the guys on my team?" Cruz slowed his speed. They had made it far enough from the tornado that the danger was over.

"I'm afraid you're about to tell me."

"When one of my men forgets his mission or they think they can't hack it in the field, there isn't time to call up their moms and dads and ask for a hug. I tell them leaders are born on the field. When they are in the thick of it, it's only them and the men that have his six. You do the hard work because you want to be the best for you and your team. For no one else. Not even the commanding officer. And forget about mommy and daddy. They don't factor in during war. If a man or woman thinks too much on the battlefield about wanting to make their parent proud, they end up dead. Take these damn pictures for you, babe. And no one else. Not even that needle prick director of yours. Just be proud of yourself."

"You have all the answers."

"Not all of them, but a few." He flashed that charming smile, but she ignored it.

"You think you have them all and you never miss a chance to tell me." She stared out the window. The fields flew past as miles racked up, putting a big distance between her and the spot she almost had success.

"Are you seriously going to pick a fight with me because I carried you back to the car?"

"You could have given me another five seconds."

"You would have been taken. Why can't you see that?"

"And why can't you see that you can't control everything? How did a man who needs to have a firm grip on everything in his life end up working with weather, the most unpredictable thing in the universe?"

"Do you know what I think the most unpredictable thing in the universe is?" Anger rocked his voice.

"I can't imagine." She didn't even bother to hide the sarcasm.

"Women."

CHAPTER 10

WITHOUT A CAMERA, chasing any more tornados seemed pointless. Ayla's soul hurt. She should tell Cruz to turn the car around and go back to Aurora instead of this wild pilgrimage for another camera. Time for her to admit defeat, but she didn't want to do that after his male pigheaded comment about women. She also didn't want to admit defeat because then she would have to call her director and listen to his male pigheadedness.

"We'll circle back to Radiant. I thought I saw a pawn shop on the main drag. I'll get you another camera." Cruz changed lanes and passed a car going too slow in the left lane.

"Is that a guilt gift?" She should quit while she was ahead, but her mouth continued to run into unwanted territory.

"I'm sorry for what I said." He pulled off the

interstate and took the long road lined with trees that would dump them onto the main street of Radiant with its abandoned buildings and forgotten stores.

"Thanks."

"I'm not replacing your camera because I feel guilty. I want you to succeed."

"Then why do you continue to argue with me about how I do my job?"

"Because I want to protect you. Is that so hard to believe?"

"I don't need you to protect me." But she did. At least for now. She needed him to be here so she wouldn't panic and if she did, which she clearly already had, he was the only person she wanted to be with when the bad things happened. That was why she had called him to come for her.

"I know that. And it's not my job to protect you any longer. We're going our separate ways when this is all over. I'll keep that in mind. Okay?"

"Yeah... okay." She fiddled with the radio to fill the space with something other than this conversation. She had subscribed to satellite radio to keep her company on the long drives across state lines so she wouldn't have to figure out where the local stations were. The expense was a guilty pleasure. The classic rock station played a song about being too deep in love. She shut off the radio.

"I'm sorry too. I may have stayed too long at the

edge of the tornado." It hurt to admit that. She had been so close she had forgotten about her panic for a second. It was as if her chest had opened wide and she could fly right alongside the monster storm. But she owed him her honesty—most of it anyway.

He arched a brow but spared her the I told you so's. "Can I ask why you only brought one camera with you? I thought you owned at least three."

She couldn't look at him because the answer was embarrassing, so she opted to stare out the side window to reply to his question. "I sold my other equipment to pay bills."

It hurt to admit that too. She had tried to hold off for as long as possible, but between the baby and Cruz leaving her, she hadn't worked in months. Bills piled up from the hospital and just life in general. Every time Cruz asked her if she needed money, her pride said no. She didn't want him to think she was falling apart without him, even if she was. So she sold her equipment and kept the lights on.

"Why didn't you say something? I would've helped you. In fact, I had asked you about money."

"I didn't think my husband, who wanted to divorce me, would be amenable to loaning me money. Remember, we hadn't had that sex in the motel room yet. I assumed your opinion of me landed somewhere around repulsed."

"Jesus, Ayla. I never felt that way about you. I also never wanted you to worry about money. I didn't want to cause you any more pain by making you struggle. That's why I always asked about money. I thought maybe you had saved some I didn't know about. If I had known…"

"Could you stop being a good guy? You're like a damn Boy Scout." She began to forget what she was so angry about where he was concerned. When he said things like that, the pain diminished.

"I kind of am." He shrugged with a devilish smile. "Are you sorry we made love last night?"

"Are you?"

"I have no regrets about last night. I hope you don't either."

She did not. Not a single one. In fact, she would do it again, if given the opportunity. Instead of saying any of that, she needed to change the subject and get on safer ground. When this was all over, then they could talk about the tough stuff like the possibility of trying again or the finality of their relationship. She needed to stay focused on her task and whether she liked it or not, her task appeared to be purchasing a new, or at least new to her, camera.

The road opened up with the trees falling away. Radiant remained the desolate town that raised the hair on her neck. With the sun dipping lower and taking any brightness from the gray sky with it, the abandoned buildings and sparse houses were coated in a layer of dinge.

"I didn't like this run-down town. Do we have to be back here?"

"We didn't see all of it. Maybe off the main road is nicer." He offered her a smile and she found herself smiling back. Cruz could charm her into anything.

"I saw enough." The place gave her the creeps last night. Much like the town of Sugar had as well.

What kind of person lived in the town with one traffic light that creaked on its hook in the wind? Where more buildings were boarded up than not? Where the residents didn't seem to be? She had seen other small towns like Radiant while chasing, but none of them made bumps grow over her skin.

"Radiant was closer than the town we just ran from. We'll see if they have a camera at that pawn shop and get back on the road."

"I'd like to get out of these wet clothes, and I'm starving since we didn't stop for breakfast." She hadn't realized until that moment how hungry she actually was or how cold her skin had become under her wet garments.

"I'm sure one of the rooms at the motel is still available. I think we were the only ones there last night. I didn't see any other cars." His clothes were still wet too. His t-shirt outlined the hills and valleys of his pecs and chest.

"See? It's creepy."

"It's just one of those small towns that folded after the interstate came through. We'll be fine for a few hours. You can grab a hot shower, and we can get some food before we go to the pawn shop."

"Thanks. I'll try not to allow my mind to wander away with itself, thinking about stories involving chain saws and shallow graves."

"You need to stop watching those true crime shows." He choked out a laugh and her heart tapped her on the shoulder. She was a goner for this man.

"Never, Lacerda. I love me some good serial killers." She laughed with him this time and the tension from earlier ran off her skin like rain on river rock.

She grabbed her phone and checked the radar maps. One storm cell was due to pass through this area tonight. It might possibly turn into a tornado. If it didn't, maybe it would be fierce enough that she could edit the film just enough to make it look as if it were.

Television was hardly reality. If she gave her director something to work with, even if it wasn't the actual thing, maybe she wouldn't lose her job.

She stole a glance at Cruz as he focused on the road and navigated back to the motel. The parking lot was still empty, but the diner had a few cars filling spaces. Max's Hash House was lit up like a carnival. People sat in booths, eating and talking.

The neon sign on the roof blinked to welcome travelers in. How many came and never left? She shook those crazy thoughts away and focused on something more positive.

He pulled around Max's and parked by the motel office with the other neon sign that read Vacancy. No surprise there that rooms were still available. Who would stay in this place if they didn't have to?

"Do you want to come in with me while I get the room?" Cruz turned off the car.

"I'll wait." She didn't want to go inside that office and talk to the woman behind the counter.

"I'll be back soon." He unfolded from the seat, but she grabbed his hand before he could get out. "What's up?" He looked back at her.

"Be quick, okay?"

"It's going to be fine." He gave her a quick kiss and closed the door, leaving her inside with her thoughts.

She hadn't noticed the sandy-colored paint of the motel that was streaked with black lines as if dirty water had poured down the side, staining it. The doors to the rooms were actually a faded blue that last night she mistook for light gray.

She pushed out of the car and stretched. The air smelled of rain that wasn't coming down in Radiant. But the thick clouds in the sky told a story of rain to come.

Cruz stood on the other side of the office window, chatting it up with the woman who had dark wavy hair to her thick shoulders. Cruz must've said something funny because the lady tilted her head back and laughed. She smacked the counter a couple of times too. That was Cruz, making friends everywhere he went.

She walked away from the office and past a few of the doors on the first floor. Cruz was right about being proud of herself. He was always right and it was damn annoying. Would it have been so bad to have a father who loved her for who she was and not always wanting her to be her brothers?

Cruz had stopped loving her for who she was. Last night had been amazing, and he might even remember how he felt about her before their lives went to hell, but what would stop him from leaving her again the next time she did something that was completely and utterly her?

A vending machine took up a small alcove tucked in between rooms four and five. She would kill for a candy bar and had money in her wallet in the car. She turned back.

Her thoughts wandered away from worries about Cruz to those true crime shows she liked so much. Each episode drew her in with their mysteries and whodunits. It was always the spouse. She wondered why anyone still tried to murder their husband or wife these days. They always got caught. Watching on her sofa, under a blanket, it was as if she would remain safe from life's real horrors. But that wasn't true, was it? Real life horrors had fallen across her life too. Just different ones.

She opened the car door and fumbled around in her messy tote bag. Her wallet had to be there somewhere.

"Howdy," a male voice said from behind her.

She jumped and a small scream fell out of her mouth.

"Sorry about that. Didn't mean to scare you none." A man with long, stringy salt-and-pepper hair, wearing a Navy baseball cap stared at her. His hands were dirty as was his white undershirt that revealed skinny arms.

She stared back, unable to get her mouth to work or her feet to move.

"Hey, are you okay?" He peered closer with narrowed eyes.

She tried to step back, but her legs banged against the open car doorframe. "I'm fine. Can I help you?"

"Looks like you might need some help. You're not from around here. Are you lost? I can give you directions." When he spoke, his lips pulled back into a face, revealing a mouth without many of its teeth.

She stole a glance at the office window. Office

Lady and Cruz shared another laugh. She wished he would hurry.

"I don't need any help. Thank you." She wanted him to go now, but he wasn't moving.

"I'm not trying to scare you, ma'am. This isn't a town for tourists. Nothing to see here any longer. You and your friend would be better off finding a Hilton somewhere." He pointed to the office.

"Were you following us?"

"No, ma'am. Saw you last night at the Hash House and then again right now pulling in. A young couple in these parts is an unusual sight, is all. And I know all the residents. You ain't one of them. What brings you by?"

She didn't want to say any more about what they were doing. He took a glance in the car and saw the laptop hooked up to the dashboard.

"What's that stuff in there?" he said.

Cruz came out of the office just then. The smile on his face fell off when he noticed this guy speaking with her and was replaced with a darkness across his face, but he quickly returned the smile. He placed his hand on his hip, as if he might be looking for his gun.

"Do you need some help, buddy?" Cruz stopped inches from the man and stood his full height with his chest up. He angled his body and relaxed his knees. That smile didn't reach his eyes.

"Not me. I thought maybe you and your lady friend were lost." The man took a step closer.

"We're good. Thanks." Cruz didn't move. She held her breath.

"I didn't mean no harm." He held up his hands.

"I'm sure you didn't." Cruz didn't move.

"Name's Roddy. You former military?" Roddy adjusted his Navy baseball hat.

"What makes you say that?"

"I can always spot one. Did my time in Vietnam. You've seen some battle too, haven't you?"

"I have. Retired. Air Force."

Roddy stuck out his hand. "Sorry to scare the missus." Cruz shook.

Roddy turned to her. "Apologies, ma'am. I come on too strong sometimes. Not used to seeing new faces. But like I said, not much to see in this town. I wouldn't stick around long."

"Thanks," she said.

Roddy gave her a wave and ambled through the parking lot toward the Hash House. He looked back over his shoulder one more time before turning the corner and disappearing out of sight.

"What was all that about?" She checked to see if Roddy had returned, but he was gone as if he'd never been there.

"I think he was just trying to be helpful. For some guys, civilian life never fits right again. He doesn't know what to do with himself, if I had to guess. Did he scare you?"

"A little." She didn't want to be mean and was being judgmental, but his uncleanliness and missing teeth freaked her out.

"Told you. It's those crime shows." He cracked himself up.

"Do you think he'll come back?" She checked over her shoulder again. Still no sign of Roddy.

"I doubt it. Let's go. We've got the same room as last night."

Cruz unlocked the door and let her in first.

"Rue down in the office said the cleaning crew hadn't arrived yet. She figured we wouldn't mind sleeping on the same sheets." He tossed their bags on the floor.

The bed was still unmade. Even the pillows had the dents their heads had made. She worried this room would haunt her, and here she was back in it with all the memories of their lovemaking. She was really beginning to dislike this town.

"Do you want to shower first?" he said.

"Do you mind?" She kicked off her shoes. For a split second she thought about asking him to join her but squashed the idea. They needed to talk first before they jumped into bed again.

"Save me some hot water." He winked.

The towels were still untouched as neither of them had showered before they hurried after the storm. Her skin was gritty and dirty from standing near the tornado, trying to take its picture. Her stomach ached with the thought of what she had documented and what she lost when Cruz had grabbed her. But he had to. She would have been killed.

She turned the water up high and stripped out of her damp clothes. The motel provided a couple of travel size bottles of body wash and shampoo. Fancy for a place like this. She had her own stuff in her bag but didn't want to go back out now that she was naked. Cruz would think she was coming on to him again. Though she wouldn't mind another go at him, she wanted to be clean first.

Hot water ran over her skin, soothing the tightness in her muscles. She tilted her head back in the water and soaked her hair.

The bathroom door clicked open. "Did you need something?" she said without looking behind the shower curtain.

"Did you bring any soap? I can't believe I didn't pack any," Cruz said.

"I have some in my bag, but I'm using the one the motel supplied. I can't believe you forgot to pack soap too. That's not like you." She lathered the soap between her hands. The sweet smells of honey and flowers tickled her nose.

"We weren't going to shower on the hike."

"Are you sorry you missed it?" She peeked

around the curtain. He stood there without a shirt. His torso was sculpted with muscles that ran down to the waist of his pants. His dark chest hair tapered to his navel. At his age, he still hadn't grayed. He would look good either way, because guys were lucky like that, but time hadn't caught up to him yet.

"Only a little, but not because I'm with you. The hikes clear my head." He narrowed his eyes. "What are you staring at?"

"You."

"Why?" He fisted his hands on his thin hips.

"Why not?" She pushed the curtain to the side, giving him a full view. "Want to join me?"

CHAPTER 11

No RED-BLOODED MALE who liked women would turn down Ayla's offer. He would be an idiot to say no. She stood there in her full naked glory, unbridled.

Cruz ran his gaze over her curves. The water covered her body in glistening rivulets. His tongue wanted to follow the path the water made.

"Don't think, Cruz." She pushed the curtain to the edge of the shower rod..

But he didn't know any other way except to think through all the pluses and minuses to what would happen if he stepped in that shower with her. They had already made love and it messed with his head. She nearly got herself caught in a tornado today. Every fiber in his being jumped into red alert as that massive wind tunnel had come toward her. He could not lose her, but they still had some mountains to climb together.

"Getting in there with you means something," he said—because it did. Loving her had always meant something.

"I know. It means we are still attracted to each other and maybe when this chase is over, we'll work things out. Maybe we won't. Maybe when we're not facing tornados or sleeping in a crappy motel, we'll decide we like being apart. But for now, in this moment, I'm cold standing here with the curtain open. Either join me or not, but I'm closing the curtain and keeping the heat in." She yanked the shower curtain shut.

He stepped out of his pants but hesitated. He might be making a mistake, but it was a mistake worth making. He pulled back the curtain.

"That's better." She ran her soapy hand over his shoulders and his chest, stopping before she hit the good stuff.

"Let me." He took the bottle of liquid soap from her. "Turn around."

She obliged him. He always loved watching her walk away from him when she was naked. He couldn't get enough of her backside. He lathered his hands and rubbed her back. The shower smelled of flowers and he wished they were in a field surrounded by tall grass so he could love her against the earth, the way he liked to best.

"That's nice." Her voice came out in a purr. He was hard before his hands went anywhere but her shoulders.

She moved her hair to give him more access to her neck. He massaged the soap into her smooth skin, taking his time in the places she would be most tight. Steam filled the space around them, but he didn't need the extra heat, not around Ayla.

She leaned into his hands and he pressed harder into her muscles. He brought his lips to her neck to taste her sweetness.

She turned to face him. "Let me wash you. Turn around, please." She made a spinning motion with her hand.

"Whatever you say."

Her hands found his shoulders this time, and she kneaded her fingers into his aching muscles. A groan slipped from his lips. He hung his head, taking the massage deeper. Hot water ran over him.

"This is the best shower I've had in a long time," he said.

"Me too." Her hands slid down his back, taking their time as they went. She lingered along his spine and then worked her hands into his lower back.

"How does that feel?" she said.

"Good."

"Just good? I think we need to change that." Her

hands found their way to his front, and she cupped him.

"Better than good." His words were hoarse and distant, as if someone else had said them.

He turned and kissed her hard. She tasted brilliant, and he needed more because he had been starved of her for too long. Cupping her face, he tilted her head back and took the kiss deeper. He wanted all of her. Her tongue wasn't enough. Her hands on him weren't enough.

He reached for her most intimate place, the place she had given him before all others. He didn't give a damn if she had taken a partner while they were separated. She had the right, but he would never stop loving the fact he was her first and no one, not any other asshole who tried to take his place, could claim that. Together, they would share that memory of her first time—only them.

She wrapped her legs around him, and he pinned her against the shower wall.

"I don't want to wait any longer." She held his gaze with her lust-filled one.

"Are you sure? There's no rush if you need more time." He could control himself long enough to make sure she was satisfied.

"I need you to hurry." She nipped at his lip.

"You're in charge."

He thrust himself inside her, and she let out a little cry which only made him harder. He held her tight as they moved together. Each stroke obliterated his brain like a massive wind blowing out power lines. His power was hers now. She would own his heart even if they couldn't find a way to stay together. He would never be free from the hold she had on him, and he didn't care. Not about anything but the two of them joined together, the pressure building inside him, and the taste of her on his tongue. Even their disregard for a condom again could not deter the call to his heart. In a month, he may regret his foolish abandon, but for right now, the only thing he wanted was to have all of him inside her.

She leaned her head against the wall and called out his name as he brought her to the end, her muscles flexing against him. He could not wait another second, try as he might, but gave into the release and followed her.

When he was done, she slid from his waist and wrapped her arms around him. He rested his chin on her head while their hearts beat in perfect time together. The water ran cold, and he didn't give a damn if he froze to death in this spot.

"Are you good?" he said.

"Can you take me to bed and warm me up?" She stared at him with mischief in her eyes.

He tucked a finger under her chin and kissed her nose. "What about dinner instead?"

"Are you asking me out on a date?" The smile on

her face radiated like the afternoon sun. It's ultraviolet index a ten and ready to burn him from too much exposure. That light reflected in her eyes as she tilted her head back and laughed.

She turned off the water and handed him a rough towel that did little to dry him off. He would ask her out anywhere if he thought what just happened was a commitment.

"Just dinner." He stepped out of the shower and held a hand out for her. She didn't take his help but brushed past him out into the bedroom. "Ayla, wait."

"No promises. I get it. You wouldn't want to break a promise, and you don't trust me."

He didn't know what to say. She could always see into his heart. "It's not that—"

"Save it, Cruz. When this is all over, we'll talk. Until then, we'll screw when we get the chance. The sex is pretty good. We can't deny it. Get dressed and buy me dinner. I've earned it."

"I CHECKED THE RADAR. The storm cell seems to have stalled out." Ayla plopped a fry in her mouth and savored the salty grease. She had been eating like crap for too long. It was going to catch up to her. As soon as she returned home, she'd go back to running. Another good thing about living with

Cruz was he was her workout partner. He never let her sit too long before he dragged her out for physical activity.

Max's Hash House was quiet tonight. Only one man sat hunched over the counter, slurping on whatever was in his bowl. He would look up at the television mounted on the wall in the corner, then back at his bowl. She pulled out her phone and snapped a photo.

Cruz scrunched up his face. "What was that?"

"I want to know what that guy's story is. I took a picture." She put her phone back in her bag.

"Better not let him see you." Cruz dunked a fry in ketchup, then shoved it in his mouth.

"Will you protect me if he gets mad?"

"Of course I will," he said with his gaze on his food.

He hadn't even blinked when he said it, as if it was as natural as severe weather. She needed to stop thinking about all the good things Cruz did, and she would start right after she wiped the ketchup off the corner of his mouth with her thumb.

He grabbed her hand and wrapped his lips around her thumb. The heat of his mouth made her head spin.

"Mmm…" He rolled his eyes into the back of his head.

"You might want to control yourself, Lieutenant

Colonel. People might see you." She didn't pull her hand away, wishing he would do it again—everywhere on her.

He released her and the heat floated away like a rotating supercell. "Let them look," he said.

"Wow. That's a first. Public displays of affection aren't exactly your thing." Other than holding her hand, he rarely showed too much affection outside of their home, unless he was drunk. Then he might kiss her.

"I'm taking a page out of your book."

"Since when?"

He leaned over the table and whispered in her ear, "Since you hooked your legs around my waist in the shower."

"I thought you said this was just dinner and not a date." She tamped down the excitement brewing but still hoped that they could forgo the painful conversations waiting for them and jump back into just being in love the way it was before. Her whole life was divided into before the accident and after.

He flopped back down in his seat. "You're the one who said we could screw."

When would she stop being so vulgar? "Figures you listened to that."

The waitress came over and placed the check on the table. "No hurry. Have a good night."

She was a different waitress from yesterday. This woman was tall and thin, almost as tall as

Cruz, with long strawberry-blond hair to her waist that she clipped back in a square barrette. Her round face was full, and her earlobes hung in a droop almost to her neck as if she had worn heavy earrings all through the eighties. She might have been stunning once, but time dulled her sparkle.

"Do you know if the pawn shop is still open?" Cruz pulled his wallet out of his front pocket.

The waitress checked her watch. The women who worked here should wear name tags.

"I think for another thirty minutes. Smitty never locks the door on time. He doesn't have anywhere else to go, but you didn't hear that from me."

"Thanks." Cruz handed her some cash. "Keep the change."

The waitress, who resembled a less attractive Nicole Kidman—no offense to the waitress— smiled as she looked at the money. She must've performed a quick math equation and realized Cruz had left a large tip. Another Cruz thing to do. He was perfect. It nauseated her. No, it didn't.

"Ready?" he said to her.

She hurried out of the booth. "Very."

He took her hand and led her outside. The humidity had hung on like a drunk uncle at a funeral, waiting to be thrown out. Summer's long day held out for a final few minutes, but night was ready to take over and had practically won that battle thanks to the dense clouds.

"A storm is coming," Cruz said.

"Radar says it might not materialize into anything. I don't think we're going to get lucky tonight."

"You will. It's coming." He stared up at the sky.

The American flag blew in the wind across the street at the gas station that sat in the shadows of one light over a single pump.

"You're sure?" She didn't need to ask. He knew. He always did and that was one of the reasons she wanted him with her on this trip. Her last meteorologist would have relied on the radar and told her to head home, nothing to see here.

"Of course, I am. Let's get that camera while there's still time." He took her hand again, and she let him because her connection to him did not diminish.

They walked down the street instead of taking the car. The pawn shop was only a couple of blocks down, and they both needed to stretch their legs. They passed the post office and the police department. On the opposite side of the road was a boarded-up store, but the sign above it read *Steve's Insurance. He's got you covered.* Looked as if Steve found something else to do.

No cars drove down the road. A bat flew above them, a dark silhouette against the ever-graying sky. Darkness would swallow them up soon. She wanted to be back in their dingy motel room with the door locked and Cruz's arms around her. For the first time, she didn't care about the pictures or her job. Radiant's main street, she didn't even know if that was its name, didn't welcome them with open arms. Its arms were crossed over its chest, waiting for them to leave.

"This is it." Cruz held the door open for her.

Smitty's pawn shop looked like many pawn shops across the country. She had been in a few as a seller and a buyer. The place smelled like wet paper and dog and was packed to the hilt with objects people wanted out of their lives for a few bucks.

Glass cabinets made an L shape and inside those cabinets were the kind of valuables better left behind a locked door, or someone with sticky fingers might find it in their possession. Engagement rings from former lovers glimmered at her. Gold pocket watches from Grandpa's armoire nodded a stoic hello.

Ayla wasn't sure, couldn't know, but took a guess that the man behind the counter helping a customer was none other than the Smitty mentioned by Nicole Kidman's look-alike in the diner. Smitty's brown face was creased with years of experience around his eyes and mouth. His gray beard speckled his jaw and his large hands pulled something off a shelf behind him. The man being helped reached for it.

She recognized the greasy hair and blue cap. When the man turned around, she would be certain his mouth would be missing some of his teeth. Roddy was buying something. Hopefully, not a firearm or a hatchet.

"Ayla, come take a look at this." Cruz waved her over to a spot in the corner where a smaller glass cabinet sat below a leather motorcycle jacket and an antique tea set.

She hadn't noticed that Cruz had walked away and went to join him. She needed to pay better attention to her surroundings.

"Would this one do?" He pointed to a Nikon in the cabinet. It was an older model, but still digital which was a blessing since she didn't have any film on her and doubted old Smitty with his large hands and double chin had any either.

"Beggars can't be choosers." An old saying her mother always used. She owed her mom a phone call. It had been a month since they spoke last. Mom would be thrilled to hear she spent a few days with Cruz. If Ayla decided to tell her that much. They didn't share secrets and watch movies together like other women did with their mothers and daughters. After she lost the baby, her mother pursed her lips and said Ayla was her own worst enemy. Maybe she was. Maybe her mother was right.

"Does that mean it's no good?" Hurt filled his eyes.

"I'm sorry. I didn't mean to sound like an ungrateful bitch. It's perfect."

"If it isn't, I can find another place. I thought I saw a Walmart from the interstate."

"No, the camera is fine. I don't want to get back in the car, anyway. I just want to go back to our room. It's been a really long day and this place smells funny." She checked over her shoulder to make sure her voice hadn't carried. More than the smell bothered her.

"I'll get the owner." He turned from her, but she grabbed his arm.

"The guy from earlier is here. Did you notice?" She stood on her toes and leaned in, getting as close to his ear as she could.

"I did. He's fine, babe. Just an older guy who's probably lonely." Cruz squeezed her arm.

"How can you be so sure? He gave off a weird vibe earlier and kind of looks like a character in a B budget horror film." She allowed her mind to run away with itself again.

"I smelled him."

"You did what?" She burst out laughing. Cruz laughed with her and their voices carried. Smitty and his customer turned in her direction.

"I'll be right with you." Smitty raised a bear-sized hand.

"Hey, it's the couple from the motel." Roddy walked over.

"Now look what you did with your sense of humor. I hope that nose of yours is right," she said. She had to remind herself she was safe with Cruz, and he had promised to protect her always.

"Do you remember me? I'm Roddy," he said, standing beside them.

"Roddy, nice to see you again. I don't believe we introduced ourselves properly the last time. I'm Cruz and this is my wife, Ayla." Cruz's smile never faltered.

She wrapped an arm around Cruz's waist and pressed against him, needing to feel something solid and secure.

"Sorry if I scared you earlier. Let me make it up to you." He pulled out a deck of playing cards and shuffled. His fingernails were covered in dirt. "I'll do a magic trick."

She didn't want to see a magic trick from a man who didn't spend enough time on personal hygiene, but to be polite she nodded and pretended to be interested.

Roddy asked her to pick three cards and shove them back in the deck in any spot. She hesitated to touch the cards but didn't see a way out of the trick without being insulting. He fumbled with the deck.

Her gaze never left his dirty nails. After a minute of searching, he showed her all three of her cards were next to each other and in order.

"Clever," she said. It was even if it was bumbled. With a little practice and a good bar of soap, Roddy might be ready for an open mic night.

"I'd tell you to enjoy your evening, folks, but if you stay in Radiant, that might not be the case."

"Are you trying to run us out of town? What did we do to you?" Once again, her mouth had a mind of its own.

"Ayla," Cruz warned.

"Don't let old Roddy here scare you nice people off." Smitty lumbered over and took his place behind the glass case with the camera. "He worries over nothin'."

"My old joints don't lie. A terrible storm is coming like the one in '08. Going to wipe out this town for good this time. If I were you, I'd get back in that car and head as far west as your gas tank will take you."

"Why are you still here?" she said.

"Nowhere else to go. And these people of Radiant need someone to organize their where-abouts during and after the storm. 'Night, Smitty. Get downstairs soon." Roddy pointed at Smitty, then walked outside. He looked to the sky, adjusted his dirt-crusted baseball cap, and limped away.

"Don't pay no mind to Roddy. He hasn't been

the same since he came back from Vietnam. He means well, but he doesn't know when to stop flappin' his gums." Smitty croaked out a laugh. "Pun intended. There won't be a storm tonight."

"I think Roddy might be right," Cruz said.

"Nothin' on the weather service," Smitty said.

"Let's call it a hunch." Cruz shrugged.

"Well, then I'll be sure to find a safe place right after I lock the door tonight. Now, what can I help you with?"

"If it gets bad, do you have a basement or an interior room with no windows? I'm serious about this, sir."

"He knows what he's talking about. He's a meteorologist," Ayla said.

"Really now? Thank you for your concern. You may be gettin' your job wrong. I listened to the weather from some of the truckers on the CB. That storm stalled out. Not coming this way." Smitty laughed, but it quickly turned into a cough that bent him in half.

"Are you all right?" Cruz said. "Can I get you anything?"

Smitty shook his head and coughed two more times. "Worse thing I ever did was quit smokin'. Haven't stopped hackin' a lung since. Doctors don't know what the hell they're talkin' about. Or scientists." He winked and pulled a yellowed handkerchief from his back pocket, wiped his face, and returned the dirty square to its original spot.

She was going to need another shower and to gargle with disinfectant after this.

"Now, tell me what had your eye in the case?"

Besides the camera, there was also some jewelry, a gold framed mirror, an antique brush set, and some baseball cards.

"Sir, there is a storm coming. Please trust me," Cruz said, ignoring Smitty's question.

Smitty looked out the window. Night had grabbed hold of the day and shoved it out the door. The wind continued to blow, but that was all.

"Thanks for the concern, son, but I've lived in Radiant my whole life. I know when a storm is comin'. Was it the camera the lady wanted?"

Smitty pulled the Nikon out of the case and handed it to her. It was heavy in her hand and didn't fit the way her newer camera had. But the battery was charged and the buttons seemed in working order. She pointed the camera at Cruz, finding just enough light to highlight some of his chiseled features and shadow others. If this were her camera, she would snap that photo of his serious look and frame it.

"What do you think?" Cruz said.

"It will do." She handed it back to Smitty.

"Come on up to the register. I'll ring you up." Smitty lumbered away with the camera.

"Thank you for the camera." She squeezed Cruz's solid arm.

"This will all work out. In an hour or two, you should be able to get some good photos, if you promise not to tempt fate too much."

He went to the register and paid for the camera. Smitty handed it over in a plastic bag. "You all come back now, you hear?"

"And you get to a safe place if you hear the tornado warnings, okay?" Cruz said.

"Roger that." Smitty laughed and broke out into another coughing fit. He waved them out the door and went into the back.

"I think I saw an ice cream stand one more block up when we came in. Do you want to grab some before we head back?" Cruz took her hand again.

"That little yellow place with the Cream King sign on its roof?"

"Yeah. It looked like an oversized shed, but I saw some people in line. Feeling adventurous?"

"When am I not?" Being outside again had settled her nerves. They weren't far from the motel if the weather kicked up, and she could check the radar for any changes. Or Cruz would tell her. He could grab dirt from the ground, shake it out of his hand, and without anything but his instincts, he would know.

They walked up the block. The Cream King was

surrounded by a field and trees behind that. One streetlight cast a cone of warmth on the building and gave just enough brightness to see by.

The trees swayed in the wind, rustling their leaves like long claws clicking on asphalt. The shed like structure sat alone, away from other businesses on the main drag. On a sunny day, this would be a peaceful spot to enjoy a cool ice cream cone with a loved one. Patrons might even be able to forget the worn down town of Radiant for a little while if they looked in the direction of the trees, but tonight without a moon or stars to light the way, the darkness was an ominous reminder she and Cruz were alone and outsiders.

The parking lot to the Cream King was made of gravel and weeds. A few faded and worn picnic tables sat waiting for someone to join them. Another parking lot and storefront without anyone in it. The ice cream stand was closed for the night. A *see you in the a.m.* sign hung over the wood board that covered the opening where people must stand in line to order.

Cruz dropped down onto the bench of the picnic table. Names of people who had sat at the bench and reminder dates from long ago were carved into the tabletop. He pinched the bridge of his nose and squeezed his eyes shut.

"Are you okay?" She sat beside him and gripped his knee.

"Yeah. I think so. A headache came on out of nowhere. Maybe too much salt at dinner."

"Could the barometric pressure be dropping?" The hairs on her neck stood up. "Cruz, we need to get back."

He held her gaze. "It's too soon."

"Your timing was off." Familiar panic weaved its way out of her belly, ready to press on her chest and stifle her air. They had no shelter, nothing to hide under that would keep them safe from bad weather. Nothing to protect them.

He stood and searched the sky. Lightning flashed down out of the clouds. Wind thrashed through the trees.

"The storm should be miles away," he said.

"It's right on us? How? Like it followed us or something?" She needed to run, but her feet wouldn't move. Frozen in place, her brain's commands short-circuited.

"A fierce cell of weather will do whatever it wants whenever it wants. We don't control the weather. It controls us. And this storm is coming straight for us."

A loud, high-pitched screech came from their phones and broke the night wide open.

"It's the emergency service warning." Cruz pulled his phone out of his pocket and held it up for her to see.

The yellow triangle with a black exclamation

point was too late. She already knew what they were up against. That warning was for others. Hopefully, they heeded it.

"I have to get footage." She fumbled with the plastic bag, trying to pull out the camera.

Roaring wind with footsteps as heavy as thunder pounded through the trees again. This time the wind bent the thick trunks like tall reeds in a swamp. More wind whipped her hair across her face. She fought to push it away. Lightning continued to split the sky in two and cast a glow on the monster after them.

A wide rotating funnel grew out of the woods and reached for the sky. The storm was upon them and had arrived without warning like a stalker climbing in a bedroom window.

"No time for you to get pictures. We need to move." Cruz grabbed her hand and ran.

CHAPTER 12

THEY NEEDED TO FIND SHELTER—AND fast. Cruz held on to Ayla's hand with all that he had. If he let go, she would fall behind, and he couldn't allow anything bad to happen to her. Trying to outrun a tornado was insane, but he had to try. He hoped they weren't too late. Him and his stupid idea to go for ice cream. He should have insisted they return to their room. They might have an edge, though, if the funnel slowed and stayed in place as it sometimes could. That would be terrible for everything around it, but they would have a fighting chance.

Their feet pounded the pavement as they ran past the pawn shop. Smitty stood outside looking at the sky in their direction.

"Get inside," he yelled above the wind.

"What?" Smitty yelled back, stepping away from the storefront.

"Go back. Get inside. Now. The tornado is here." He didn't know if Smitty heard those last words, but he couldn't stop to find out. Hopefully, Smitty would realize those guys on the CB had miscalculated and he would find shelter.

"Cruz, I can't make it." Ayla's voice carried over his shoulder, but he didn't look and risk slowing them down.

"Keep running, damn it, and don't let go." He squeezed her hand harder and tugged her forward. She only needed to stay on her feet. He didn't want to stop and throw her over his shoulder, but he would if she couldn't keep up with him.

The wind was on their heels. Paper and light debris flew through the air. Dirt and dust coated them as they ran. They needed shelter, and they needed it now. The motel wouldn't be safe enough, but it would have to do.

Max's Hash House came into view. The inside lights were still on and people remained in their seats by the windows. If the tornado came through here, they would all suffer. They needed to be away from the glass. Hadn't they heard the warnings? Why weren't they hurrying home to their loved ones?

Someone stood at the diner door, yelling to the patrons. As he and Ayla closed the space, the figure came into view—Roddy. He directed people to their cars.

"Get them inside," Cruz said and slid to a stop. Ayla bumped into him from behind, but he caught her before she could go down on her rump.

"I'm telling them to go home," Roddy said above the wind. His stringy hair blew off his neck. His hat came off his head and Roddy slammed it back down.

"It's too late for that. Is there a basement here?" Cruz stopped a man and a woman from coming through the door. "Stay inside and away from the windows."

"We want to get back on the interstate," the man said.

"You won't make it," Cruz said. "Roddy, I need to know, is there a basement or not?"

"I don't think so. Never seen one."

"Then make everyone get into the walk-in refrigerator or pantry. Hurry." He gave Roddy a small shove, but the guy barely moved. He was all muscle in that skinny body.

"What about you two?" Roddy said.

"I'm going to make sure Rue is okay, and then we'll join you." If they had enough time.

"Roger that, sir." Roddy saluted.

He didn't bother to correct Roddy. In civilian life, no one needed to salute him. Once upon a time, he outranked a guy like Roddy, but today nothing mattered except getting to safety. Roddy went back inside and Cruz turned to Ayla.

Her eyes were wide as she stared at him.

"You can stay here too. It might be safer for you that way."

Wind howled and kicked up more dirt as the tornado moved in a slow and deliberate way down the street toward them. Power lines exploded as the storm ate whatever was in its path. They didn't have much time now.

"I want to stay with you."

He took her hand and ran to the motel office. Rue squatted under the registration desk.

"Come on. You can't stay there." He held out a hand.

"I'm not moving. I can't." She shook her head and put her hands over her ears.

"You've got to. Come on." He reached down for her, but she swatted him away.

"Git now. I'm fine here. Git." Rue kicked him.

He tried one more time to pull her up, but she was big with a lot of strength. She gave him a hard shove, and he flew backward, hitting his head on the shelf behind him.

Ayla helped him to his feet. "Leave her. If she wants to stay, we need to get out of here."

They ran toward the motel rooms. He tried some of the doors on the first floor, but they were all locked. There was no time to make it back to the diner. He tugged Ayla up the steps to the second floor and fumbled for the keys to their room. He unlocked the door with shaking hands and shoved her inside as the power went out.

Ayla screamed.

So did the wind.

"The bathtub. Now."

CHAPTER 13

AYLA COULDN'T SEE her hand in front of her face. The motel room was pitch-black. The wind screamed and shook the building on its foundation.

"Cruz, where are you?" Panic blocked all reason. It was happening again like before. The tornado would carry them away, tumbling them head over feet until they were broken and battered.

She had driven alone that night. Rain had belted her windshield in a nonstop beat. Everything in front of her blurred between the rain and the oncoming headlights. The wipers worked overtime and could not keep up with the inches of water hitting the car. Her stomach cramped with each yard she drove. She was in over her head, but it was too late to back out.

Her weather radar hadn't been in real time because she couldn't afford the latest equipment that constantly updated. Her phone was old and the apps weren't working. What she did have, had refreshed every five minutes.

She should have turned back thirty minutes sooner, pulled over, or stopped even, but she hadn't. She had taken a risk instead, and her risk had been a mistake.

Cruz's voice had filled her head with words like plan, take precautions, double-check. She had wanted him with her in that car, and she had almost called him, but she needed both hands on the wheel to keep the car on the road. The call would have to wait. And when it came, it hadn't been from her.

She had followed the road, thinking she would be able to get ahead of the tornado, but the road had ended. Just stopped. Her only choice had been to reverse out of there, losing precious time. Driven by a force that controlled her, she kept going. But she shouldn't have.

The tornado had changed direction when she was too close. She had no idea because her information was lagging. The draft had slammed into her, and the car had tumbled. She hung upside and suspended in her seat. Time had slowed. Rain burst through the broken windows. Dirt was in her mouth. Something hit her arm. She landed in a ditch and the car rolled twice more. She didn't remember anything after that until she woke up in a hospital, no longer pregnant.

"Babe, I'm right here. I've got you. It's okay. Don't scream." Cruz pulled her against his strong body, and she was no longer fighting for her life in a broken car but needing to find shelter with the man she loved.

"We might not make it," she said. What if she lost Cruz this time?

The windows rattled as the wind tried to get inside.

"Come on." He pulled her away from the windows. A door banged opened. Cruz rustled around behind her. His phone lit up the bathroom.

Her breath slowed. "My phone." She had it in her pocket, forgotten. She yanked it out and turned on the flashlight feature too. "My battery is low. I didn't charge it."

"I'm good for a while." He rested the phone on the sink with the light pointing down, then closed the door. "Get in the bathtub."

He didn't wait for her to respond and picked her up, placing her in the tub. He climbed in after her and wrapped his big body around hers. She was pinned between the porcelain and him. She didn't want to think about the last time this tub was cleaned as her face was against the bottom.

"I don't want to die." She had done this to them. She had risked her life a second time and now his.

The tornado had come for them, as if it stalked them and cornered them in this bathtub.

"No one is dying today." He didn't move.

The weather had other ideas. As if a giant stepped down from the sky and gripped the motel's roof with both hands, sending it flying into oblivion. Wood cracked and split, glass shattered. The motel shook as the wind swept in and pummeled them with debris. Rain fell on them, soaking them. A loud crack, ten times as loud as any thunder roar, hurt her ears. A boom shuddered their little bathroom. Something large landed outside the bathroom door.

"Cruz, make it stop. I can't do this. I can't stay here. I have to get out of this bathtub." She squirmed against him, struggled to get her body out from under his, but he held on with strength she didn't know he had.

"It's okay, babe. It's okay. Just stay put a little longer." His voice was calm. His hands were in her hair. His hips pinned her waist. His legs forced hers down. She couldn't move if her life depended on it —and it did.

"I can't. I can't. Make it stop." She squeezed her eyes shut, but images of Cruz in battle, holding a teammate down from running straight into fire played behind her eyes. She only had those images because he had told her. He had seen destruction like this up close. Her man who showed her his heart, was also a machine who reacted without emotion.

Something hit the wall with a crash. Cruz's phone skittered across the floor. Lightning lit up the bathroom in quick intervals. Rain continued to pour on top of them and filled the bottom of the tub, wetting her face.

"Cruz, I can't breathe." She was going to drown. This is how they would find them, with Cruz on top of her and her submerged in three inches of water—dead.

"It's just a little rain. You're fine. There's plenty of air. Hang on." But he let up on his hold.

She tilted her head, trying to see above them. Only half of the roof was torn away, but the rain continued. Something flew past the opening in the roof.

"Don't look," he said. "It's almost over."

She didn't ask how he knew. He just did. Maybe the wind was dying down. She couldn't tell. Her ears rang, and her brain screamed out for help. The bathroom still shook on its foundation as if it would tumble away or maybe that was just her.

After another few minutes, Cruz released his hold and sat back. She struggled to her hands and knees. He stepped out of the tub and helped her stand.

She brushed her hair away from her face and looked around. Wood and drywall covered the floor. Pieces of insulation flapped in the wind. The sky was now their roof.

"Is it over?" she said.

"For now. I need my phone." He pushed broken plaster and beams from the ceiling out of the way.

"Cruz, my God, you're bleeding." She lunged for him.

Blood caked the back of his head and ran down his neck. He put a hand to the wound and pulled it away with blood on his hand.

"I'm fine."

"It's a head wound."

"I'll be okay. Try the door and see if we can get out." He went back to looking for his phone.

She tried the sink first to clean out the wound for him. Nothing came out of the faucet when she turned it. "We don't have any water."

"Try the door, Ayla. We need to get out of here, and I doubt we can climb out of the roof. This structure isn't going to stay put."

Her hand gripped the knob and turned it, but the door didn't budge. She threw her hip into it and still nothing. "It's stuck. Something is blocking it. It must be whatever caused that loud bang."

"Probably a tree. Got it." He pulled his phone free from behind the toilet. He touched his hand to his head again and winced.

"We need to take care of your head."

He put up a hand to stop her. "We assess the

situation and find a way out. Search and rescue. We triage later. I need you to follow me until we're safe. Can you do that? No arguments."

His eyes were stone-cold. He was in military mode now. She would do what he asked. He would be the way out.

CRUZ'S HEAD THROBBED. His heart beat in the wound. Warm blood ran down the back of his neck and soaked his shirt. Head wounds always bled a lot. It was probably nothing, but he might have a concussion. He wasn't sure what clocked him, but most likely a beam from the ceiling. At least Ayla was unharmed.

His fingers hit all the wrong spots on his phone. He needed to make a call and couldn't get his hands to work right. Taking a deep breath, he tried again and went into his saved contacts. Mason's number was the best thing he'd seen since this shit went down. He doubted Mason or Ryder were anywhere with cell service, but he had to try. He needed help because no one except Rue knew where they were. If she had stayed under that desk, he suspected she was hurt or worse. He and Ayla could be here for days before anyone found them. They didn't have days. She was falling apart by the second.

The phone rang and rang. Voicemail would pick up any second.

"Lacerda, what's going on?" Mason yelled into the phone.

Relief washed over him. "I didn't think you'd answer."

"Why wouldn't I answer when I see that my best friend in the world is calling? I can't let those kinds of calls go to voicemail. That would be rude." Mason burped on the line.

"Hey, I thought I was your best friend," Ryder said from somewhere behind Mason.

Shuffling noises echoed through the phone as if someone moved the phone away. "You are my first best friend. He's my second," Mason said to most likely Ryder.

"Mason, listen, man, I need your help."

"Did you and Ayla have a fight? Ryder and I can come and get you."

"It's not like that. We're in trouble. Can you get off the trail?"

"Trail? Oh, no. We never got on the trail. Said fuck it. No offense. Once you left, we changed our minds, didn't see the point, didn't feel like sleeping in the woods in the rain or cold. We're too old for that shit, man. We came home, and now we're hanging at Ryder's place. Had a few beers. When are you coming back? What do you think about starting a street hockey league?"

"Mason, shut up and listen. Ayla and I are at the Max's Hash House motel off Route 70 in Radiant, Kansas. We're trapped. A tornado came through. I don't know if anyone knows we're here or when a search and rescue team in this town can get to us. I repeat. We can't get out. This structure won't last. Can you come for us?"

"Shit. Give me a second. I need to clear my head."

"What's going on?" Ryder said in the background.

"Shut up, Callahan. I'm thinking."

"He's thinking," Ryder said in a singsong voice into the phone.

"I can get a chopper from the Brotherhood. Logan Bishop is a pilot. He's got that copter he calls Roxy because of the call sign on the side. I saw him around The Centre with his buddies Nash and Darius before we left for the hike. I'll give him a call." Mason sounded more like himself.

"What if he isn't there?"

"I'll figure it out. How hard can it be to fly a helicopter?" Mason laughed and burped again. "Sorry."

"Pull your shit together and try not to get yourselves killed trying to save us."

"Don't worry about us. We'll be there as soon as we can. Are you hurt?"

"Superficial head wound on me. Ayla is okay.

Bring a medic bag just in case." His head started to spin. He wasn't sure how superficial the wound was, but he didn't want Ayla to worry. She was already a wreck.

"Roger that. Can you send me your coordinates? We'll land as close as we can."

"Coming now. I'm hopping off to preserve my battery. Call me when you land."

"Stay safe, brother. And watch that fat head of yours."

"Thanks. Hurry." He ended the call.

"Are they coming?" Ayla looked at him with wide eyes. Her skin was gray, and her hands shook.

"Looks like they changed their minds about the hike when I left to come to you. Lucky break. They'll be here as soon as they can." It wouldn't be soon enough for him.

Rain continued to come in from the hole. He pulled the shower curtain off the rod and wrapped it around her like a poncho, covering her head. They sat in the corner as far away from the hole in the roof as possible. His long legs took up too much space when he stretched them out. His feet touched the tub. Ayla hooked her legs over his. It wasn't comfortable, but it would do.

He placed a part of the shower curtain over himself too, then applied pressure to his wound with a towel. The blood should slow soon. Then he'd be all right. He had to be.

"How long before they're here?" Ayla said.

"They'll be here as soon as they can." He sure as hell hoped it was sooner than later, but he didn't know how long it would take to find Logan and fire up his helicopter. If Logan didn't have the copter preset for takeoff, then it would take longer for them to get off the ground. And if Logan wasn't around, who would fly? Mason and Ryder sure as hell couldn't fly a helicopter. They would have to find someone else at the Brotherhood. There had to be at least one other guy who could fly a chopper.

His head hurt, and the room spun every few seconds from the pain. He couldn't pass out before they got here. He had to protect Ayla. The worst might not be over.

"What do we do now?" She pressed against him. Her warmth seeped into his cold skin.

"We wait."

CHAPTER 14

AYLA'S BODY ached from sitting in one place too long. She tried to shift to get some feeling back into her butt and legs, but she didn't want to disturb Cruz. He had fallen asleep—or worse, passed out. She wasn't sure which but prayed for the first.

Her eyes had adjusted to the dark. But it was still hard to make out the details of anything.

Cruz's phone was in his pocket. She didn't want to fumble for it—again disturbing him—but she would love to know what time it was or how long it had been since Cruz spoke to Mason. Would they be able to fly in? Where was the storm now?

No one had come looking for them. She had no idea how bad the damage was around the motel. The whole town could be gone. Had anyone survived, if that had happened? What if everyone was dead? What if Mason and Ryder couldn't find them?

She made a fist, sinking her nails into her palm to stop the crazy thoughts from happening. They would be fine. She had to keep telling herself that. But what if they weren't? What if this was the end?

Cruz stirred beside her. The shower curtain crinkled as he moved. "Hey, beautiful," he said.

"Hey. I'm glad you're awake." She placed a hand on his face and walked her fingers over his beard. She wished she could see his eyes better, but it was still too dark.

"How long have I been out?" He shifted.

"I'm not sure. A while."

He pulled out his phone. The light from the screen saver—a picture of a sunset—cast a glow into the room. The new light eased some of her worries back into the shadows.

"Looks like it's been about thirty minutes."

"Is that bad?"

"I'll be okay. Don't worry." He turned the flashlight back on and swooped the light over the room.

Nothing had changed. Beams still sat lopsided, hanging from parts of the roof. Plaster and wood littered the floor. Wires hung from the open ceiling. At least the rain had stopped for now, and the power being out was a blessing with the exposed wires.

"Can I check your head?"

"I'm good, but thank you. I'm going to try the door and see if I can tell how secure the walls are." He sat up straighter but groaned and leaned back. The phone slipped out of his hand and landed by his leg.

"You're not good."

"It's just a little pain. I've been through worse." He climbed to his feet. The shower curtain fell away from him. He swayed and gripped the sink as his legs folded under him, sending him to his knees.

"Please stop lying to me. You're hurting. I need to know how to help you." She guided him back into a sitting position.

"Shock." He slurred the word.

"What?"

"It's shock. Did my head stop bleeding?" Some of his words came out as if his tongue had tripped over his teeth.

Shock? What did she do for shock? Had she read somewhere the victim needed to be kept warm? She bit back the panic, churning in her belly. She needed to hold it together for him. If she fell apart, they would be in a bigger mess.

"I need your phone to see better. I have to reach over you to grab it. Is that okay?"

"Don't try any funny stuff, lady. I'm not in the mood." A laugh rattled around in his throat, but it turned to a cough.

"Save the jokes and your energy." She inspected the wound with the flashlight. It glistened with blood, but it didn't seem to be still running down his neck. The blood on his skin had dried to a dark brown.

"How bad?"

"It might've stopped bleeding, but it's not scabbing." She took one final look.

"Need staples, probably." He took the towel and put it back on his head.

She turned off the flashlight so she wouldn't point it in his eyes by accident. "Did you change your passcode?"

"Why? You want to see if I have naked pictures of other women?" He tried to laugh again but groaned. "This fucker hurts. What the hell hit me?"

"I don't know. There's so much garbage in here and it's too dark to see. Passcode, please."

"It's the same. I never changed it. What are you looking for?"

A warm flush ran over her body. His passcode was the two digits of her birthday, two digits for the day they met, and two digits for the day he asked her to marry him. She wished she could go back to that day. Almost any day besides this one would be good.

"I want to see how long ago it was you spoke to Mason."

"Not long enough. They have to find Logan, get

to the Brotherhood compound, and take that helicopter up. And if they're dealing with weather, it could add to the time. We're on our own here."

"We need to try and get out."

"I'll try the door." He went to sit up.

She pushed him back down. "Not you. I'll go." She turned on the flashlight again and handed him his phone. "Point that at me, please."

Cruz did as she asked. She navigated the mess on the floor and stepped over a hammer. How the hell did a hammer get up here? But that was what wind could do. A tractor trailer could have landed on them. She tried the door, but it wouldn't open.

Something let out a long, painful groan. It took a second for the sound to register. The bathroom's outside wall crumbled inward over the bathtub as if it were a sandcastle. She panicked and jumped to get out of the way but tripped over a fallen piece of wood and landed on Cruz. He let out a whoosh of air.

A pipe broke from inside the wall and squirted water all over them like an open fire hydrant. Water poured out in glugs, filling the bathtub. The night sky offered a little light as if to tease them with a glimpse of the outside world they might never get to see again.

"I thought the water didn't work." She pushed to stand, careful not to use Cruz for stability.

"It's a main pipe in the wall." He climbed to his feet and swayed.

"Can you stay upright?" She wouldn't be able to carry him if he passed out again.

"I'm going to have to."

"What do we do?"

"I don't know."

CRUZ FORCED his mind to work, but it fought him every step of the way. He was definitely going into shock. He was probably already there, but he needed to stay focused until the guys got there. He didn't know how much longer he would last, though.

They couldn't climb down without a ladder. They couldn't get out of the door because of whatever blocked it. They could scream for help, but that wouldn't do a whole lot of good.

"What do you mean, you don't know what to do?" Ayla said.

"I'm sorry. We're stuck."

The water continued to fill up the tub. Soon it would spill over and start filling the floor if the main line wasn't shut off. Which it probably wouldn't be if no one was around to notice. Maybe the water would only get to their waists. Ayla could stand on the toilet for extra height. But he didn't know how much longer he could stand at all. He really wanted to sit right now.

"What are you saying? Are we going to die here?" Her voice climbed a few octaves. He needed her to stay calm.

"No one is going to die. You need to keep your head about you, okay? Panicking is how lives are lost. We'll figure something out, but in the meantime, help is on the way."

"Okay. Okay. I'm sorry." She flapped her hands as if she might take flight.

"Don't be sorry, babe. Let's just think." It hurt to think. His knees buckled, but he caught himself before he fell.

"Sit on the toilet. You can't stand." Ayla guided him over, and he didn't argue.

His bruised male pride had to surrender. Better to admit he was the weakest link. "I'm not much of a protector, am I?"

She brushed some of his hair away from his face. The tender touch crushed his heart. "You're my protector," she said.

He took her hand in his. "I need to say something before I pass out completely."

"You're not going to pass out."

"I might. I want you to hear this in case I do."

"You're scaring me a little." Her laugh came out forced. He knew her full laugh and wished he could hear it one more time.

"I love you. I've always loved you. From the moment I laid eyes on you, I knew you were the woman for me. I'm so sorry I left you after we lost the baby. If I could go back and do that over, I swear to God I would. I'd never leave you."

The sky beyond the broken wall took a spin. He closed his eyes to keep upright, but he must not have done a good job if Ayla's screams were any indication.

CHAPTER 15

AYLA SHOOK him and begged him to wake up. She held his head against her belly so he could remain sitting. She would stand that way for as long as it took. He couldn't fall on the floor. The water would be over the side of the tub soon.

"I don't know if you can hear me, Cruz, but I'm going to talk anyway. You know me. I'm a nervous talker. I guess I think the bad time will pass if I talk right over it. That always drove you kind of crazy when you were studying."

She stole a glance at him. He hadn't moved. She held on.

"I love you too. I've always loved you. I dreamed about the idea of you long before you showed up that day on campus. I never told you this, but my friend Julia had seen you first and wanted to ask you out. I couldn't let her do that because I knew you were going to marry me."

Cruz stirred. "Ayla?"

"I'm right here."

He eased out of her embrace. "I'm okay. I am."

"You're not." The tears fought their way out. She tried to hold them back, but her lip quivered and she lost control. "I'm sorry. I'm crying."

"You don't have to be sorry." He held her hand.

"I'm sorry for everything," she said.

"I'm the one who should be sorry. I should have kept you safe after the accident, and I didn't. I left you alone when you needed me most."

"You were hurting too. I should have been there for you. You had lost the baby too. I didn't think about your pain." She had been selfish, putting her needs above his. At the time, she couldn't think about what he needed or how what had happened affected him. All she could see was the red-hot pain of loss coating everything she looked at until she couldn't see straight any longer.

"It was an accident."

"I should have listened to you, and I'm sorry that I didn't. I should have given you the one request you had and not chased while I was pregnant. It's no excuse but I still felt as if I had a lot to prove, maybe more since I was pregnant, but I ruined our lives with my selfishness."

He pulled her into his arms. She sat on his lap

and rested her head on his shoulder. The water spilled over the side of the tub and splashed on the floor. She was cold and wet and tired.

"I'm sorry I lost our baby." The tears poured as fast as the water through that pipe that was threatening them. Her body shook with sobs. The moans of pain came from her.

What had she done? She harmed her own child. It was all her fault. She cried for their baby and for their marriage.

"Shh. It's over." He rubbed her back.

She wiped her nose with the back of her hand. "Do you think he'll be waiting for us someday?"

"Our baby?"

"Yeah. I want to get a chance to see him."

Even though their child hadn't been full term when they lost him, and she didn't know for a fact that it was a boy—it was just a gut feeling—she pictured him as a toddler. He would have Cruz's dark skin and deep brown eyes. She could see him with a back-and-forth sway to his walk as he navigated the world on his chubby legs. She imagined that serious look with the turned-down brows when he tried to figure out something just like his daddy. She could picture him laughing and running into her outstretched arms, and he would smell like sunshine and promises.

She hoped there would be a day when she could see him again and tell him how very sorry she was for what she did. And hopefully, he would forgive her for her stupidity.

"If you want to see him someday, you will."

"What about us?" She had to know. Finding out couldn't wait any longer.

"I want us. All of us. Broken. Bruised. I want to do my life with you. If you'll have me all over again." He kissed her and she kissed him back, trying to put all her apologies and all her love into that kiss so he would know with certainty how she felt.

"I never want to be without you," she said.

"Then it's settled. When we get out of here, we'll start over." He brushed a curl away from her face.

"Cruz, the water is covering your feet." She stood up. Water continued to pour out of the pipe, but the tub could not hold any more. Water lapped over the side like the ripple of a lake. Only this wasn't any serene lake. Trouble chased them.

"I know. I didn't want to say anything, if you hadn't noticed."

"Will they get here in time?" She looked to the sky as if the helicopter would appear and they would be saved.

"They're trying. We just have to have faith."

"I don't want to die now that I have you back." She gripped his shirt in her fists. The unfairness of it all, to finally say the things she had wanted to say for months but had been too scared to before now.

She had Cruz back and they might not make it through the night.

"Do you know how brave you've been through all this?" He leaned his head against her belly.

"Hardly." She didn't want to think about the number of times she had lost it in the past two days.

"You're brave. You were afraid to come out to chase storms and you did it anyway because you have integrity and you keep your promises. You convinced me to join you. That was brave."

She couldn't help but laugh at that one. "You can be scary when you're backed into a corner."

He looked up at her. "Me? Nah. You can chase as many storms as you want. I won't get in your way again. I won't tell you how to live your life. I just want to be a part of it."

"I'm done chasing after this. I'll figure out something else." She never wanted to be in this situation again and she never wanted to see him hurt like this. She'd be happy taking photos of puppies and babies with bows on their heads.

"Ayla?" He leaned his head against her again.

"Yes?"

"I think I'm going to pass out again."

~

THE WATER WAS at her ankles, and it was cold. It sloshed over the sides of her shoes every time she moved and soaked her socks. Cruz's phone had died thirty minutes ago. No one could reach them and they still didn't know where help was. Her legs ached from standing in one place, but there was nowhere to go. Cruz needed to stay seated. At least now he was awake.

His appearance concerned her. His eyes were lackluster and when she touched him, his skin was cold and clammy. He hadn't complained about any pain, including his head, but that was him. He could be having a heart attack and he probably wouldn't tell her. Still, she'd take the absence of complaints as a good sign.

"I'm thirsty," he said.

"We have plenty of water. Just nothing to drink it with." The water in the tub looked clean enough.

"Better if I don't drink any right now."

"How are you feeling? Are you nauseous?" she'd asked him that a hundred times since this whole thing started and each time he said he was fine. He wasn't.

"I'm feeling better, but I don't want to take any chances. I do wish I could lie down or lean back, but sitting on the toilet will have to do. Just keep talking. It gets my mind off my head."

"Okay, you asked for it. I think this is a ghost

town and all the residents have either left or died here."

"We saw plenty of people around. I'm pretty sure they weren't the walking dead." He moved his feet through the water. It soaked the bottom of his pants.

"We think we saw. But we don't know for sure, do we? What if the whole thing, the people in the Hash House and that strange man Roddy, were in our imaginations?"

"Both of our imaginations? At the same time?" He snickered.

She cracked up with him. "I'm losing it."

She leaned against the sink to ease some of the pain in her legs. She was almost ready to sit in the water just to get off her feet. She tried stretching her quads, but it did little to relieve the discomfort.

"What's going to be the first thing you do when we get out of here?" he said.

"Sit in the hot sun, drink a whole lot of wine, then take a nap. What about you?"

"Make love to my wife." He glanced up with a smirk.

"Always trying to one-up me, aren't you? So competitive." She plopped a kiss on his cool lips. "Are you sure you're okay?"

"Are you going to keep asking me that?"

"Probably."

"My head hurts and I'm cold. Better? How are you holding up?"

"Same. Minus the head injury. When are they going to get here? The waiting is killing me." She couldn't stand still any longer. If she could see over the broken wall, maybe someone would be down there and they could yell for help. She had to do something besides stand in this dilapidated room, waiting to be saved.

"Don't get too close to that wall," he said.

"I just wanted to find out if I could see down to the ground. Where are the people of this town?"

"Helping others. Mason and Ryder are coming. It's just going to be a little longer."

She leaned her knees on the edge of the wet tub and drenched her pants. The wall was still too far away to see over. If she could get closer...

"Ayla, come back." He reached for her.

She moved away from the tub's edge and held out her hand. The floor shifted under her. She fell away from Cruz. Time slowed. Water splashed her in the face. Something caught on her shirt and scratched at her skin. Her arms windmilled, trying to keep her balance, but she dropped into nothingness.

And screamed.

Cruz dove from his seat and gripped her wrist like a vise just before she tumbled to her death. Her legs dangled below her, searching for something to stand on, but never quite getting there. The floor had given way. The motel room below her, the inches of water, and the tub were all she could see.

"Hang on." He tried to pull her, but she continued to swing in his hold. "I can't get too close. The floor might give way more."

"Don't let me fall." She stared up at him, helpless. His grip crushed her wrist, but the pain would pale against falling into what waited below.

"You're not going to fall. Just keep looking at me." He gripped the edge of the sink and sank to his knees. "I need you to reach up to me with your other hand."

"I can't. I'm going to fall. Please don't let me fall." She glanced down at her feet, kicking back and forth in the empty space.

"Look at me, babe. Just keep your focus on my face, okay? Don't look down." His voice snapped her gaze up.

"Will I die if I fall one story?" She couldn't remember how far someone could drop and still live.

"Look at me, Ayla. Only at me. That's it, babe." He smiled at her as if this were any other day. He was the kind of man anyone would want in battle with them. He was the kind of man she wanted with her.

"My hand is slipping." Her skin was slicked with sweat. He wouldn't be able to hold her.

"I've got you. Reach up with your other hand. Now."

"I can't."

"Now, Ayla. I need you to do this, babe. Just reach up." Tears filled his eyes.

She closed her eyes and gritted her teeth. With strength she didn't know she had, she swung up her arm. Her legs kicked, dragging her away from Cruz, but he clasped her wrist tighter. Her fingers grazed his arm and latched on.

He heaved, grunting and groaning, then fell back on his ass in what was left of the water and dumped her on top of him. More of the floor gave way where he was kneeling only seconds before. They were pushed up against the wall by the toilet. They barely fit, but there was nowhere else to go.

"This is it. We're going to die here." She held on to him. From the moment they had crossed the town line into Radiant, something evil came for them. Maybe it was all in her head, but from the looks of their situation, she had been right. They weren't going to make it out alive.

"I'm sorry I don't have a way out of here for us. We should have gone inside the diner with the others." He held her close, tucking her head under his chin.

"It's too late now to think about the what-ifs. Believe me I know." If she could turn back time, she would have a thousand times already. She would have gone back to the day she left to chase while pregnant. Or back to the moment when she knew she should turn around and find a motel for the night instead of taunting fate in that reckless way she had. Or to the time when Cruz had asked her not to leave. To stay with him, in their home, together all night when his heart had been broken because of her. She had chosen not to comfort him when he had asked in his quiet way. They wouldn't be here now if she had just once made a different choice when it counted.

"I've played the what-if game in my life too, especially in the Air Force. It doesn't work, but it doesn't stop me from spinning the past in my head. I was relieved to leave battle. I haven't told anyone that. It's one of the reasons I took that promotion to Lieutenant Colonel. I didn't want to be in the thick of it anymore."

"I was glad you took the promotion too. I wanted you to come home safe and sound, even if you weren't coming home to me." She pressed against him, needing to be as close as she could. These would be their ultimate moments together, and she wanted his presence to be the final thing she felt.

"I'll be coming home to you every night now."

"What if we don't make it? I have so many regrets."

He took her chin between his fingers and tilted

211

her face toward his. "Hey, no regrets. We make mistakes. They suck and that's life. We learn and we move on. I'm coming home to you from now on. We focus on that."

She snuggled back down, and his strong arms held her tight. She didn't want to argue during their last time together. He had to say they would make it. That was what he would tell a soldier, dying in battle. They stayed huddled together for a while.

"This wasn't how I pictured this trip," he said with a chuckle, breaking the silence.

"Me either. Cruz?"

"Yeah?"

"I'm afraid." Knowing when the end was near was worse than not knowing. Living in ignorance to her final demise allowed her to take for granted that she would wake up the next day and all the things that were wrong in her life would right themselves. Finding her way back to Cruz again and then losing her life on the heels of that was unfair. Hadn't she experienced enough unfairness in this life?

"If we're being honest, I'm scared too. I don't know how to fix this, and they should be here by now."

"But I'm glad I'm with you."

"If this is the end, then at least I'm with the person I love most." He kissed the top of her head.

They sat that way for another few minutes. She was too tired to talk. Dawn would be cresting soon, and they would be awake close to twenty-four hours by then. She wanted to close her eyes and sleep. If she went in her sleep, that would be better than falling to her death. But the end wouldn't come quickly in her sleep. They would dehydrate and starve first if the whole building didn't collapse around them before that.

Wings thwapped in the distance, splintering the night silence, as if a flock of birds took off for better parts. How nice it would be to fly away with them. She imagined she was one of those birds, and she was going home—to a home she hadn't known in a long time filled with love and happiness.

The birds flew in their direction, the knocking of their wings growing louder. She wanted to tell them to stay away. It wasn't safe here, but she kept her eyes closed and rested against Cruz's chest. She was on the precipice of sleep and this moment might be the last peaceful one she would ever get. She could sink deep into the fatigue and forget if those birds would fly away and take their clapping wings with them.

"Do you hear that?" he said.

"Birds." Lots of birds. Maybe owls since it was still night.

"Not birds. A bird." He eased her away from him and looked up.

She groaned with the absence of his arms around her but followed his gaze with her own.

"Look." He pointed to the sky.

"I can't tell what it is." Something large, too large to be a bird, flew toward them. Its lights cast a beacon of hope through the darkness. She didn't want to believe what she was seeing. It had to be a mistake. Helicopter blades sounded off in the joyous rhythm of a rescue song. She tried to stand, but Cruz pulled her back down.

"It's not safe. Stay put. They'll drop a ladder down."

"It's them?"

"It's them, babe. They came for us." He leaned his head back and closed his eyes. "Thank God."

"How will they know they can't get to us any other way? Like with a ladder or something. Wouldn't they land first? Should we signal them?"

"They'll know. They're my teammates. I trust them with my life—and your life too."

The helicopter hovered above them with deafening blades. Fierce wind kicked up the dust and dirt, stinging her eyes. Her hair blew across her face, and she wrangled it behind her ears.

The lights blinked twice as if to say hello. A rope ladder tumbled down near them, but not close enough to reach up and grab. A man scurried toward them feet first. As he made his way down, she recognized Cruz's old friend. Her friend too and a surge of ease washed over her.

"I heard some punk needed rescuing. Kids today," Ryder said and shook his head. His wavy brown hair blew in the helicopter's wind.

He was a big guy with lots of muscles and would be able to help Cruz get into the helicopter when she wouldn't. Tears stung her eyes again.

"Good thing I have a friend with a helicopter. You ready to get out of there?" Ryder said.

"Boy, am I glad to see your ugly face," Cruz said. "I'm not sure if the rest of the floor will hold. You need to take Ayla first."

"Can't we go together?" She looked between Ryder and Cruz.

"Ayla, I won't let anything happen to that dumb husband of yours. He owes me dinner for the last bet I won."

"You two are so calm." Her insides hummed like a race car engine. She was ready to jump out of her skin and neither man had broken a sweat.

"All in a day's work." Ryder unhooked a full-body harness from his belt that she hadn't noticed before.

Another rope with a large hook descended from the helicopter, and Ryder hooked the two together. Someone above lowered it farther, within reach, and Cruz grabbed it.

"Babe, I'm going to help you get in this, and Mason will pull you up." Cruz assisted her as she slid her arms in and hooked the harness around her waist and legs.

Cruz scrunched up his eyes and cursed.

"Is our fearless leader injured badly?" Ryder said.

"Head wound," she yelled back up, then turned to Cruz and placed a kiss on his lips. She gave a thumbs-up to Ryder who turned around and offered one to the helicopter.

"I love you." She kissed him again. She would never stop kissing him if they truly made it out safely.

"Love you too. I'll be up in a minute." He smiled with a weariness that reflected in his dull eyes.

"Thank you," she yelled to Ryder as she passed him.

"Always glad to help." Ryder gave her another thumbs-up.

She kept her gaze on Cruz, injured and still sitting on that floor. She hated leaving him behind. He looked up at her and never blinked. Even with the distance growing by the second, the strong connection they shared didn't alter. Why hadn't she noticed that before? His face would always be the last one she would want to see each night before she went to bed.

He gave her a quick wave as she entered the helicopter, then he was out of sight. Mason and two other men she didn't know were there. The pilot, Logan, glanced over his shoulder and nodded.

"Nice to see you, Ayla." Mason helped her out of the harness and sent it back down to Cruz.

"Thank you for coming." She threw her arms around his neck.

"Hey, now. We don't do that kind of stuff on a mission." Mason eased her away.

"I know what a softy you can be, Mason. This is me. I've known you since you were a teenager."

"Yeah, well, don't go blowing my badass cover."

"I have to see him. He's hurt and might not be able to help himself." She peered over the edge. Ryder never left the ladder. He was saying something to Cruz.

"He's good," Mason said, turning her gaze away from Cruz. "He's done this a hundred times."

A thunderous crash echoed below them. She turned to see Cruz suspended near Ryder and the rest of the motel disintegrating below them.

CHAPTER 16

CRUZ CLIMBED INTO THE HELICOPTER. He was wet and hurting. His head pounded, and his vision blurred in and out, but he had never been happier to see his longtime friends. Ryder slapped him on the back. Mason punched him in the shoulder.

"That was close," Ryder said.

"No kidding." If they had arrived for him and Ayla five minutes later, the ending would be very different.

"If everyone is inside, I think I'll hit the road," Logan Bishop, the pilot, said. "The weather might not hold."

"What about any others? There must be others. Should we stick around to help?" They were body-guards after all and all former military, including Nash Melendez and Darius Ford, who were also on this helicopter.

Nash didn't look like military any longer. He had grown out his hair to his shoulders and wore rope bracelets up his arm. He was a contradiction of sorts for Cruz. Nash was one of the best snipers he had ever worked with, and he taught yoga to vets and Brotherhood Protectors who struggled with post-traumatic stress. Nash preferred the yogi life too. He had even tried to get Cruz to come to a class.

"Nash spoke with the staties on the way over," Mason said.

"I've got a buddy in the Kansas State Police who was in sniper school with me. Everyone in that diner was rescued. One woman was found dead on the scene inside what might have been the motel office. No one knew you two were in here except for us."

"Just like I thought," Cruz said. He had been concerned no one knew where they went. He had told Roddy they would come back. When they hadn't, Roddy would have assumed they found shelter somewhere safe and not on the second floor of the motel.

"When you spoke to the state police and told them you were coming, they didn't send help for us?" Ayla said.

"Well, when they heard who was on their way to you, they asked if we could do the extraction instead of them. We're better at it. I'm Nash, by the way." Nash stuck his hand out to Ayla.

"Ayla, let me do the introductions since our man, Lacerda, here isn't himself." Ryder put a bandage on the back of Cruz's head. "You just met Nash; he teaches people to shoot really far and to bend into a pretzel. This here is Darius."

Darius tipped an imaginary hat to Ayla.

"If you want to hack into any computer, Darius is your guy. Though he never does anything illegal unless Nash begs him to," Ryder teased.

"That was special circumstances. I needed a weather report," Nash said. Logan and Darius laughed. Cruz hadn't heard that story yet, but he would be asking soon.

"And our pilot is Logan. He can fly anything with wings," Ryder said.

"I hope you enjoy your flight," Logan said.

"I know I've said it before and I'll probably say it a million more times, but thank you, everyone, for coming," Tears filled Ayla's eyes. She wiped away the one tear that got loose.

His heart shouldered its way into his throat. He loved this woman more than anything and almost didn't save her. He would find ways to thank each of these men for rescuing them. Once again, he owed Mason and Ryder his life. Now, Logan too. And what the hell, he'd throw Nash in with the others. If anything had gone south, Cruz was certain Nash would have been boots on the ground like the others even though they hardly knew each other.

"How come you all came? Not that I'm complaining." He wasn't expecting to see Nash or Darius, but he was glad for the extra help.

"Darius and I crashed at Logan's last night. Long story. When Logan got the call for help, he woke us up to tell us he was going, so we came along. Logan owed me a helicopter ride anyway," Nash said.

Logan waved from his seat in front.

Mason opened the medical bag and prepared a syringe. "When we land, we'll take you to the hospital and make sure that thick head of yours is still working. In the meantime, I'll start an antibiotic for you."

"Thank you for coming. I don't know what we would have done..." He couldn't finish. His emotions clogged his throat. The words were too hard to grab from the shelf in his mind because of the pain. Later. Later he would tell them how much he appreciated them and their swift rescue. He and Ayla would not have made it without them.

"Enough of that... of whatever the hell that was about to turn into." Mason made circles with his index finger. "We came because it's our job to protect. And we came because our brother was in need."

"No man—or woman—ever left behind," Ryder said.

And they all agreed.

EPILOGUE

Two weeks later

As the summer sun took its final descent for the day, stars claimed the night sky for themselves. Cruz searched for his favorite constellations and located each before he dropped into the chair on his porch. Every clear sky brought him a good night's sleep. No severe weather meant Ayla wasn't tempted to chase. And he hadn't been tempted to hike.

He loved this little cabin in the woods away from all the noise and chaos in the world. When he came home, he was at peace, an escape from the terrors that waited around every corner. He wasn't a pessimist, but a realist. War and weather had taught him to be that way.

Fireflies blinked their cold light into the night. He had enjoyed chasing the bug and its short glow as a kid with his big brother. They would run around the backyard with glass jars, trying to capture the insects. Dante would poke holes in the lid just big enough for the bugs to breathe but not get loose. Dante was a good older brother, always having Cruz's back. He owed Dante a call. They hadn't spoken since the tornado. Tomorrow. Tomorrow he would catch his brother up on what had happened.

Cruz had hoped to teach his own children to run in the damp grass with bare feet and hold out a glass jar to capture the fireflies and their magic. He wanted to explain the scientific reason for the light as much as he wanted to watch wonder on their little faces. Or maybe he wanted to recapture his youth and blow some oxygen back into the past. Today, his aching body longed to be twenty years younger.

Cruz's head wound stopped hurting somewhere during the past two weeks. He couldn't pinpoint when, but the first time he touched the spot where the stitches were and didn't pull his hand back with a grimace was when he went for a hike. That was a week ago. The doc in the emergency room said the gash looked as if the back end of a hammer had clobbered him. Could have been. They would never know.

He had checked on Radiant's recovery after the storm. Only one dead. Amazing. Several were injured, but nothing life-threatening. They were all lucky. This time. The town wanted to rebuild. That was what Roddy had told him. He had been able to track Roddy down thanks to Darius' tech skills. Cruz had made a couple of phone calls and Roddy appeared on the line more than happy to give him the update that nothing would keep the few remaining residents of Radiant down. Roddy had also invited him and Ayla to come out and see him. Cruz wasn't in any hurry to revisit the town. Neither was Ayla. Instead, he had invited Roddy out to the cabin for a barbeque with Cruz's friends. Roddy had his trip planned for the end of August.

The front door creaked open, and Ayla glided out in her wrinkled linen pants and gauzy cream t-shirt thin enough to show her bra. He wasn't sure how he felt about the full view. She was his, and he wasn't into sharing. She had told him to shut up about it. So he had. But he still didn't like it.

She handed him a cold beer and placed a kiss on his lips. "Thought you might like this after dinner."

"Thank you." He put the beer on the porch beside his chair and would drink it a little later.

She settled into his lap, wrapping her arms around his neck. Another perfectly good chair sat empty beside him, but he would not complain about her choice of seats. He wanted her next to him every chance he could. Keeping her close to him was his main goal these days, and as long as she wanted to be in touching distance, he was thrilled.

"I'm all unpacked." She ran a finger through his hair.

"Finally. You brought the whole Aurora house with you." He placed a kiss on her lips. She tasted like beer and smelled like rain-soaked earth. She had taken a shower, and he wanted to make love to her right on the porch.

Their marital home was up for sale. It was time to leave that chapter behind them and start new.

Mason and Ryder had helped them move some of Ayla's things. Lugging furniture and bags of clothes was why his body hurt. He had given up with the chore long before she had. He had taken a short walk, then fired up the grill to make Ayla and him dinner.

"I needed most of that stuff and you didn't have anything here anyway." She reciprocated with a kiss on his neck.

"We're going to need a bigger house just for your camera equipment." His hands found their way up her shirt and rested on her back. If they kept this up, dessert would be next and on the porch, after all.

"I put out our wedding photos."

"On the kitchen table?" Like she had when the photos were ruined from the water in the basement.

"Funny. No, Lieutenant Colonel, I did not make a mess of your kitchen. I had new ones printed out, and I bought frames. I'll show you." She went to get up.

He pulled her against him. "Later. Let's just sit for a minute."

She never sat still, his wife. And he would never tire of calling her that.

"I like it here with all the trees." She pushed his shirt up and traced a line from his navel to his collarbone. Just her simple touch had the power to make him hard.

"Is it just the trees?" He took her hand and kissed her fingers.

"Nah, the sexy guy in the house was the real win." She kissed him full on, her tongue sweeping his mouth.

"I've made my decision about work," she said.

"What's that?" He hadn't wanted to push her on any decision. If she wanted to go back to chasing, he would stand behind her, even if he didn't like it —which he didn't.

They had spoken about her options some, but needed time to unwind from their latest ordeal, and she had been a bundle of nerves for the first few days back.

But when she said she wanted to move in here with him and sell the old house, they danced around her next moves. He wanted to plan a future. She wanted to let the future plan them.

"Nature. I still want to take photos of lightning and oceans and rain puddles. Coast to Coast Nature magazine is looking for freelancers. I can probably sell my stuff there. Or I can try for an exhibit in a local gallery, maybe."

"Do both, babe. You're talented enough."

"No more tornados though. Not unless I'm miles away. I could do that too, right?" Her tongue made circles by his ear.

"Of course you can. If that's what you want to do, then do it."

"I don't want to get close to the storm. Not anymore." She eased back and held his gaze with her serious one.

"I support you. Whatever you want." He leaned in for a kiss.

"Whatever?" She pushed him back and arched a brow.

"Yes. Anything at all. As long as I can get you out of those pants." He glanced down and then back at her. Linen pants with no buttons. Shouldn't be too hard.

She worked her bottom lip under her teeth. He sat back to get a better look at her.

"Something is going on in that head of yours. Spill it."

She brushed his hair away from his face. He

doubted his hair had moved, but he liked her fingers on him, and she liked the distraction.

"What do you say about trying to make a baby again?" She dropped her gaze.

He held his breath, unsure of what to say. He hadn't been expecting that one. Babies was a topic that hadn't come up since they came back from Radiant. It was too soon to know if their hasty decisions in the motel had proven anything.

He also figured she wasn't ready to have a family, might never be. He tried to accept that a life with Ayla could mean no life with children. He would do that for her, to keep her in his life. Because life without her didn't work.

"It's okay if it's too soon for you. I understand you might not want to have kids yet." She started to get up, but he held her in his arms.

"Not so fast. Are you serious about this? You want to try again?"

"I want to take pictures, and I want to have your babies. Then I want to take pictures of your babies. You haven't said it out loud, and I thank you for that, but I can tell you want some idea of what the future might look like. Are you good with my plan? Can it be enough for now?"

"That's the best plan I've heard in a long time." He carried her inside and closed the door on the fireflies and the sky full of stars.

And worked on that plan immediately.

. . .

Team Watchdog
Mason's Watch - Jen Talty
Asher's Watch - Leanne Tyler
Cruz's Watch - Stacey Wilk
Kent's Watch - Deanna L. Rowley
Ryder's Watch - Kris Norris

ABOUT STACEY WILK

From an early age, best-selling and award-winning author, Stacey Wilk, told tales as a way to escape. At six she wrote short stories in composition note-books, at twelve she wrote a novel on a typewriter, in high school biology she wrote rock star romances in her binder instead of paying attention.

But it wasn't until many years later, inspired by her children and a looming birthday, that she finally took her story-telling seriously. And published her first novel in 2013. Since then, she's gone on to publish twenty-four more so women everywhere could fall in love and find an escape of their own.

She isn't done telling stories. Not by a long shot. If you want to read her emotional and honest books about family, romance, and second chances, visit her at www.staceywilk.com

To see what she writes next, follow her Facebook group for her amazing readers – Stacey's Novel Family https://bit.ly/2FK8Lae

Or join her newsletter - https://bit.ly/2A0jEFk

BROTHERHOOD PROTECTORS

ORIGINAL SERIES BY ELLE JAMES

Bayou Brotherhood Protectors

Remy (#1)

Gerard (#2)

Lucas (#3)

Beau (#4)

Rafael (#5)

Valentin (#6)

Landry (#7)

Simon (#8)

Maurice (#9)

Jacques (#10)

Brotherhood Protectors Yellowstone

Saving Kyla (#1)

Saving Chelsea (#2)

Saving Amanda (#3)

Saving Liliana (#4)

Saving Breely (#5)

Saving Savvie (#6)

Saving Jenna (#7)

Saving Peyton (#8)

ABOUT ELLE JAMES

ELLE JAMES also writing as MYLA JACKSON is a *New York Times* and *USA Today* Bestselling author of books including cowboys, intrigues and para- normal adventures that keep her readers on the edges of their seats. When she's not at her computer, she's traveling, snow skiing, boating, or riding her ATV, dreaming up new stories. Learn more about Elle James at www.ellejames.com

Website | Facebook | Twitter | GoodReads | Newsletter | BookBub | Amazon

Or visit her alter ego Myla Jackson at mylajackson.com
Website | Facebook | Twitter | Newsletter

Follow Me!
www.ellejames.com
ellejamesauthor@gmail.com

Made in United States
Cleveland, OH
01 March 2025

14799614R00138